Ceiling of Amber

Other books by Elisabeth Ogilvie

BECKY'S ISLAND

BLUEBERRY SUMMER

THE FABULOUS YEAR

HOW WIDE THE HEART

TURN AROUND TWICE

THE YOUNG ISLANDERS

WHISTLE FOR A WIND

Ceiling

of

Amber

by Elisabeth Ogilvie

McGRAW-HILL BOOK COMPANY

New York   Toronto   London

The following authors and works are quoted in the text: on pages
19–21 and 131, Matthew Arnold's "The Forsaken Merman"; page 33,
Sigmund Romberg's "When I Grow Too Old to Dream"; page 66,
William Shakespeare's *The Tragedy of Macbeth;* and page 102,
Alice Meynell's "Renouncement."

Ceiling of Amber

1

I<small>T WAS LATE</small> afternoon and spitting snow when *Sea Dancer* splashed through the freshening chop to the Great Harry Shoal. Clarie was steering, and behind her Brian half-lay over the washboard to watch for the first buoy, long gaff in hand. The boat bucked and lurched as she struck the rough water that was the Shoal's only marker at high tide. The red buoys appeared and disappeared like the snouts of an exotic breed of seal in the swirling gray and white.

"Are they all there?" Clarie called to Brian over the sound of the engine. He nodded stiffly, as if he were too cold inside his bulky oilskins to move. He looked younger and smaller than fifteen today, and very tight, as if he were clenched all together like a fist. Maybe it was an optical illusion, she thought. She'd been staring at choppy gray water and lowering skies all day, and by now nothing looked right.

"Cheer up, this is the last of 'em!" she shouted. "Those baked beans will taste some good a couple of hours from now!"

His mouth quirked. She slowed the engine and edged the thirty-five-foot *Sea Dancer* toward the first buoy of the string they kept there. This was a rich lobstering spot which their father had always fished, and they had been

7

careful to keep traps there ever since his death the summer before, so that no other fisherman could move in on it. Clarie put the bow past the buoy just enough so that Brian could lean over the side and swiftly gaff it. His hands in wet white cotton gloves swung a loop of dripping warp around the spinning brass head of the hauling gear, and it began to wind up some fifteen fathoms of rope with a high steady whine. Clarie gave him a hand at heaving the heavy trap onto the washboard, and *Sea Dancer* jogged into the wind like a dependable horse.

"Six!" Brian shouted. "Beauties, too! Look at the broad back on that one." He held up a big dark-green lobster. Cold and weariness were forgotten as he measured each one to be sure it wasn't over the legal size, and Clarie plugged the heavy crusher claws and laid the lobsters carefully in the crate. "I don't know why it is," she said, "but the lobsters on the Great Harry are always the biggest of the batch."

"Just what every other fisherman on Bennett's Island thinks," Brian gloated, "but *we've* got them."

Warmed and revived, they approached the next buoy. They had twelve traps around the shoal, and it was possible to get almost a hundred pounds out of them. The price right now was eighty cents a pound, and Clarie's mind swam with delight. Who said Ed Tanner's kids couldn't bring in the money right along with the other fishermen?

Nobody had said it, really. They just thought, along with Margaret Tanner, that winter lobstering wasn't for a girl of nineteen and a fifteen-year-old boy. Oh, it was all

8

right for the kids to fool around with a string of traps in summer, but they should be on the mainland now, the boy in high school, the girl in that decent job she'd thrown aside like pitching a beach rock overboard. Oh, sure! Clarie thought in exhilarated anger. A woman should move right out of her home when her husband died, carting off what she could carry like one of those displaced persons, as if she didn't have a right to go on living in her own house the kind of life she was used to. Or as near that life as was possible without her husband. Clarie felt the burning of tears in her eyes, and shouted lustily at Brian as they reached for the next trap, "That's right, get her aboard!"

They were as surprised by the other boat as if a whale had suddenly blown beside them. "Hey!" Ross Bennett shouted at them. "Don't you two ever look at the weather? Get that trap overboard and head for home!"

"We just got here!" Clarie protested. Ross swung his head from side to side.

"Plug 'em and bait that trap and *move!* It's snowing harder all the time, you two chowderheads!"

Clarie looked around. Bennett's Island had been a comfortable presence five miles to the east when they reached the Shoal. Now it was almost gone behind a blowing curtain of white. Snowflakes flew by the boat to die in the gunmetal water.

"We're not leaving these unhauled," Brian said to her. "Trouble with him is, he thought he was going to get this spot when Dad died. He can't stand seeing us make anything off it."

9

Clarie didn't relay this to Ross. "Don't worry," she called to him, "we'll start home pretty soon."

"More likely an hour," Ross shouted back. "I know you two. Don't be so foolish, Clarie. Come on, I won't go home without you."

"He won't either," Clarie said to Brian, who angrily jabbed a baitbag into the trap and buttoned the door. "We're stuck with him. You want him hanging around counting every lobster we get?"

"Oh, all right! He's worse than the itch." Brian shoved the trap overboard, and took a long screwdriver to flip the belt of the hauling gear off the flywheel. Ross Bennett swung *Moonlight*'s beautiful bow toward the east, into the snow. Brian took *Sea Dancer*'s wheel, opened up the throttle, and the boat leaped forward across the small curling white crests, moving abreast of *Moonlight* and then ahead. Ross didn't bother to speed up. He grinned, and Clarie waggled her hands from her ears at him, laughed, and sat down on the engine box.

Bundled into oilskins and sou'wester, she could have been Brian's brother. They both had the same smoky blue eyes, black lashes and hair, the tendency to freckle lightly. They had strong yet fine features, but Brian's nose seemed sometimes too big, his eyes too deep-set, his jaw too sharp, just as his hands and feet were too large for his adolescent wrists and ankles. Clarie thought that one day he would be handsome, but she didn't consider herself good-looking. Men, she told herself cynically, went for the round chins, the darling noses, the soft curls, the delicate bones. At least Paul did.... For an instant a vision of the shop was superimposed on the bleak wintery dusk; right now the lamps would be lit, the draped fabrics glowing with color, and outside the windows the happy, busy people would be hurrying by. If it were an afternoon just like this in last January, Paul would be coming soon with snow on his hair and eyelashes, putting his cold hand on her cheek to make her cry out, telling her what he had planned for tonight.

"Paul, you're disrupting the staff," his mother would say, but not crossly. No one could ever be cross with Paul. "If you're so full of energy go out back and help your father open those crates." And she would smile at Clarie and say, "Don't let him walk you for ten miles through this snow tonight. I don't know what makes any son of mine such a fiend for exercise."

Oh, it had been good, and full of laughter, and in her memory always bright and warm with lamplight or sunlight. And now. . . . She blinked drearily into the dusk as the boat sped on. Then she was furious, and thought, I don't care! This is a good life! I always wanted to be a lobsterman when I was little. Why, I wouldn't go back to the mainland now even if. . . She drove herself on. Even if Paul hadn't dropped me for that simpering little idiot. . . . She looks just like that paper doll Mother saved from when she was small, and passed on to me. *Dottie Dimples.* If he showed up on the mailboat tomorrow, and begged and pleaded, I wouldn't give up this life. I wouldn't let Mother and Brian down. . . . Then treacherously, her throat began to ache,

It was getting dark fast. Brian was running *Sea*

11

Dancer at top speed, slicing through the deepening seas, taking showers of spray over the canopy windows. *Moonlight* was just a little behind. Ross, a man in his late twenties, was plainly humoring Brian. Clarie got up and stood by Brian.

"What do you bet he makes Mother another offer for the boat and gear right off?" Brian asked.

"If those darn Bennetts don't stop trying to buy us out I'll have to tell them a thing or two," said Clarie. "Especially that one over there. Lord, he's a domineering cuss!"

"He was some glad to stop us hauling around Great Harry." Brian still mourned the untouched traps.

"Oh well, maybe we'll get out tomorrow, and we've got a darned good haul here already." At last they were going up the west side, past the ghostlike dance of surf on the rough rock walls and the massive patience of the great spruces that towered high above the breakers.

With their own red and green riding lights glowing like gems, and *Moonlight*'s shining across the water at them, they rounded the breakwater where more ghosts danced in the dusk, and saw a great ball of radiance in the driving snow. It was the big flood lamp Mark Bennett lit on his wharf for nights like this. *Sea Dancer* felt sheltered water under her and sped toward the light like a bird to her nest. The tension went out of Clarie, leaving her very tired. She was glad that Ross had insisted they go home, though she'd never have admitted it.

The light shone down on the lobster car and the black water dimpling around it, and on Mark Bennett's yellow

12

oilclothes as he came down the ladder. The other lights of the village showed faintly, and wood smoke seasoned the snowy wind. *Sea Dancer* slid to one side of the car and *Moonlight* moved in on the opposite side. Mark Bennett, a big dark man, grinned at the Tanners.

"Well, if being last boat in is a sign of industry, you fellers ought to be the richest fishermen on the island by spring."

"We'd still be out there if old Granny Grunt hadn't chased us in," said Brian. Mark laughed.

"Ayuh, and the rest of them would be all groaning and reaching for their boots again, having to turn out and look for two kids when they've got their own day's work behind them."

"Seems to me two kids do a pretty fair day's work themselves," Brian said tightly. "Help me with that crate, Clarie." As she did, she knocked her foot against his in a warning not to be too mouthy. He gave her a resentful look but kept quiet. Together they swung the hundred-pound crate onto the washboard, and Ross and Mark shifted it onto the scales. There was another full crate, and one almost full.

"Well, they crawl for you, that's easy to see," said Mark. Ross lit his pipe and looked out into the dark harbor. Clarie was uncomfortably conscious of him. She supposed she should have said "Thank you" to him, but she couldn't get around it. Maybe she and Brian *were* a nuisance to the men, always having to be kept in mind. But the sight of the bills being counted into Brian's hand stiffened her. They were taking care of their mother and

13

themselves, and that was the most important thing in the world right now, more important than the job she'd left, than Paul who had left her, than high school for Brian.

"Hey, Clarie," Brian said, "why don't you go up to the house from here so she'll know we're in, and I'll put the boat on the mooring."

"You know the rule. Neither of us alone in the harbor after dark."

"Good rule," said Mark. "Awful easy to make one fatal slip out there."

Brian started up the engine and backed *Sea Dancer* away from the car. Again Clarie had that sense of discomfort. If Ross had glanced in her direction she'd have tossed something casual at him like "Thanks for the convoy." But he didn't look, and she couldn't start cold. She went forward and turned the powerful flashlight on the restless black water until the beam picked up their skiff on their mooring. Now she took the wheel and Brian took the long gaff, hopped onto the washboard and ran forward over the bow deck, light and swift as a man on a hot stove. This was the bad moment when the harbor was rough and the decks freezing, and the legs bone-tired. But tonight the harbor was sheltered, and in a few minutes the boat was on her mooring chain and the skiff alongside.

Clarie rowed. Their wharf was halfway around the harbor from Mark Bennett's big wharf. With no need of words Clarie and Brian dragged the light skiff up above high-water mark, turned it over, and tied it. Then they went past the fishhouse and across the road to their own house. The frozen ground seemed to rock under them after the long day on the restless water, and tiredness crept heavy and cold inside their oilclothes. Clarie took off her sou'wester and heard from the unseen spruce forest and the outer shores the long unbroken roar of gale and surf.

There were other houses set snugly back at the edge of the woods, but Ed Tanner had wanted to live as close to the shore as possible. The sound of the sea was always in the house, and when the sun shone on the harbor there were waves of light flowing up the walls and across the ceilings all day long.

Tonight yellow lamplight shone out, and they saw their mother's slender figure in a kitchen window and knew she was looking for them. Brian swung the flashlight in a big arc, and she waved. "Rough on her," he muttered. "Just the same. I mean, losing him makes her worry more about us."

"He wasn't drowned," Clarie answered sharply. "He could have had a cerebral hemorrhage anywhere." She felt a clutch of anxiety for no reason she could define. "He'd be proud of us, Brian! Bursting with pride, because she's living the life he intended her to live, in her own home."

After a moment he said gently, "I guess," and went on ahead of her. She had the queasy sensation of having lied. It wasn't this life their father had intended for their mother; how could it be, without him in it? But

15

did that mean that everything had to be different, that you couldn't hang on fiercely to what was left?

No, she was right, she *had* to be right. Their mother wasn't to be torn up by the roots like a helpless shrub. Paul's smile and snow-wet eyelashes danced across her vision. They were for Shirley now. "We three are all we've got," she whispered. "We have to do it this way."

2

It was from their father that they received
their height and the big square teeth and
clever flexible hands. From their mother they took the
smoky blue eyes and the curling black hair. She was
talking gaily with relief as they got out of their salt-
stiffened oilclothes. "Did you have enough lunch? I
put in extra turnovers, but I was thinking you could have
had another thermos of cocoa."

"We had plenty, Mother, honest," Brian assured her.
Out of his heavy clothes, he hovered over the stove as if
chilled to the heart. Clarie laid her hands over the teakettle's hot sides.

"Oh, bliss," she moaned. "Pure bliss, a hot teakettle.
Better than roses or chocolates."

The warm kitchen, the smell of food, the loud purring
of the cat in the rocker, the storm kept at bay—it was all
bliss. Doubts and anxieties had been left outside. Over
beans and coleslaw and hot biscuits they told their
mother about their day, and she told them of hers. She
didn't say she'd worried about them, and she shook her
head in smiling astonishment at their earnings.

"I don't know how you do it," she marveled.

"Of course the price helps," said Brian modestly.

"Don't disillusion her," said Clarie. "Let her think
we've got the special magic touch that tolls the lobsters

17

right into the traps, especially around the Great Harry."

"Ayuh, if Cap'n Bligh had left us to it."

"Captain *who?*" asked their mother.

"Oh, Ross Bennett," said Clarie. "Brian thinks he has dark designs on Great Harry. But it's just an over-developed bump of responsibility, I guess."

"By that she means he's bossy," Brian explained.

"Well, to be fair—and I have to be, much as it pains me," said Clarie, "what Mark said at the car was the truth. We'd have been the last ones in and nobody could relax while we were still out."

Brian shrugged. "I suppose so. Anyway, tonight I don't care." He lay back in his chair, patted his stomach, and smiled angelically.

"Miss Colwell wants to know how you're coming on your poetry paper, Brian," his mother said.

He groaned. "Oh, *that.*"

"Yes, *that.* It's due at the end of next week, and you haven't even made a start on it."

"Why can't I just concentrate on math and history and let that darned English go?"

"Because you'll be taking English in high school," his mother said. "And because it's your language, and you're going to know how to read it and write it and speak it."

"I can do those things already." Then he pretended to dodge. "All right, all right!" He rose up with a groan and went to get the thick book of poems. "I'll bet the ones I'm supposed to read are the longest ones in the whole book."

He leafed through the pages, glowering dramatically. His mother fully expected that by next September he'd be starting the tenth grade at Limerock High. When she was still half-stunned with the shock of her husband's death, she had given in to Clarie's arguments that the island teacher could give Brian ninth-grade work to do, so that they could spend this year at home on the island. It was to be a temporary arrangement only, as far as Margaret was concerned. But whenever Clarie thought of leaving the island, she felt as if she had crashed her face against a stone wall in the dark, leaving her breathless and aching and incredulous. Then she comforted herself by thinking, It's still too new to us all. But when Mother sees how well we can keep things going here, and admits that Brian wants nothing more in life than to be a lobsterman, then she'll accept it.

"Don't keep looking for the easiest one, Brian," she said. "What's the first one on your list?"

" 'The Forsaken Merman,' " he said in a martyred voice.

His mother looked up in pleased surprise. "Give me the book."

Clarie remembered the poem, she too had read it in the ninth grade at Limerock High. But she was not prepared for the physical thrill of hearing it now, in her mother's low voice, with the storm outside. She scooped up Hodge the cat and settled down in the rocker with him, shutting her eyes. The words went on.

> *Now the great winds shoreward blow,*
> *Now the salt tides seaward flow:*

19

> *Now the wild white horses play,*
> *Champ and chafe and toss in the spray.*

She glanced under her lashes at Brian. He was listening, his eyes bright slits in his thin face.

> *Where great whales come sailing by,*
> *Sail and sail with unshut eye*
> *Round the world for ever and aye.*

They had seen whales at a safe distance.... The story unfolded.

> *Children dear, were we long alone?*
> *The sea grows stormy, the little ones moan.*
> *Long prayers, I said, in the world they say.*

"*Margaret!*" the children in the poem called their mother. "*Margaret!*" their father, the merman, called.

> *But ah, she gave me never a look,*
> *For her eyes were seal'd to the holy book....*
> *Come away, children, call no more.*
> *Come away, come down, call no more.*

There was a forlorn silence in the kitchen, during which the wind flew violently against the windows. Then the low voice went on again.

> *She will start from her slumber*
> *When gusts shake the door;*
> *She will hear the winds howling,*
> *Will hear the waves roar.*
> *We shall see, while above us*
> *The waves roar and whirl,*
> *A ceiling of amber*

A pavement of pearl.
Singing 'Here came a mortal,
But faithless was she!
And alone dwell forever
The kings of the sea.'

Mrs. Tanner sat with the book open in her lap, her head bent over it. After a moment Brian muttered, "Corny," but without conviction. It was as if in the reading their mother had expressed a loneliness which she had never mentioned to them.

"I always loved it," she said. "When I was little it was my own poem because her name was mine. But I used to think I would never be faithless. I'd have stayed there with the ceiling of amber and the pavement of pearl." She looked at her children with a smile. "Clarie, are you going to read the next one?"

"Not after that one," said Clarie quickly. "It would be an awful anticlimax. Besides, Brian ought to go write whatever he's supposed to write about the poem, or do his math, or something."

Brian's cheekbones went red. "For Pete's sake knock it off!" he protested. "Do you have to boss all the time?" He got up. "I'm going to bed and read and listen to my radio. Anybody mind? Good night, Mother."

When he had gone upstairs, Margaret shook her head. "He's overtired."

"It was windy today," said Clarie. "It throws you around in the boat. After a night's sleep he'll sail into his work and get it all done by noon, you'll see."

"I can't help thinking it's boring for him, working

21

alone instead of being in a crowd his own age. *You* had that, Clarie."

"Yes, I did," Clarie admitted. "But look, there wasn't any need then for me to be anything but a school kid. I only had myself to worry about. Brian wants so darned much to be his own man, and the man of the house. . . ."

"He will be a man, one day. In the meantime he's a fifteen-year-old boy, and I don't want him to grow up any faster than necessary."

Clarie turned Hodge on his back and began rubbing his stomach. The conversation was becoming dangerous. She tried hard to think of a change of subject.

"And Clarie," her mother's soft voice went on, "this isn't right for you, either. You were doing so well in the shop, learning all about fabrics and decorating. There was a future for you. If I'd had any idea what was in your mind when you went back to Limerock after"— she halted, then pushed herself—"after the funeral, I'd have certainly forbidden you to leave that job."

"I didn't have it in mind when I went back," Clarie said honestly, keeping her eyes on Hodge's tiger-cub face. "It came to me all at once that what made everything even worse—if it *could* be worse—was having to go away from home. I was a little used to it, but you and Brian weren't, and the way things were—well, I just had to turn around and rush back and see if we couldn't all do something together." Her face was hot and her voice faltered, and she played with Hodge's big double paws without seeing them. But it's the truth, she argued si-

22

lently. Even if it was Paul who pushed me into it, it's still the truth that we three should be home here together.

She knew her mother was watching her and her face burned hotter, her head sank lower. She bumped her forehead against Hodge's, and he bunted back, purring ardently.

"But it couldn't have been easy to turn your back on all your good times," her mother said.

"Nothing was important enough to come ahead of my family." There was a clogging catch in her throat, but she got the last word out clearly. And that's half the truth, she thought, because even if I thought Paul was important, he didn't think I was, or he'd have never started going with somebody else the instant I was out of sight. And it wasn't as if I'd gone away to have fun!

The old angry grief rose strongly in her. I had to go home because my father died, and that's all he cared. . . . She thought for a moment that a wail of pure woe would break from her, but the strangling moment passed, and she heard Margaret's soft voice.

"All our lives have changed with your father gone. And it seems as if something has happened to my mind, my will, so I can't decide what is the right thing to do, what *he* would consider the right thing. . . ."

It was not a complaint, but a thinking-out-loud. Clarie got up and put Hodge back in the chair. "It's what I told Brian tonight," she said. "Father would burst with pride at what we're doing, keeping his traps in

23

the water and his boat off the bank, and you here." Her mother didn't look up. Absently she leafed through the poetry anthology.

"Good night, Mother," Clarie said, and went upstairs. She was glad to get into bed, to stretch out with her book and know *Sea Dancer* was safe on her mooring. She was even more glad that they'd skirted safely around the breaking ledges in their conversation tonight. Now the dangerous subjects shouldn't come up again for several days at least. Her bed felt luxurious, and she opened her book with a small sigh of pleasure.

When she began to feel sleepy she turned out her lamp and lay back in the dark. On the edge of unconsciousness she had a sudden startling vision of the lobster car as it had looked in the glow from the floodlight, of Ross Bennett standing beyond the scales, of the line of his temple and cheekbone as he gazed away from the light into the snow and the dark. She was wide awake again, uncomfortably so. I should have said something to him, she thought. I should have made myself speak. He must think we're a couple of arrogant brats.

Her pride was on fire at the prospect. She was ashamed not so much of her rudeness as of the fact that she must have shown up badly.

3

THE SNOW had stopped by morning, leaving a frosted island, and the sea a brilliant blue. Surf roared along the windward shores and beat against the breakwater.

"Well, what do you say?" Clarie said to Brian at breakfast. "How about pitching into that schoolwork?"

Brian made an ambiguous sound and took second helpings of everything. Clarie and her mother went upstairs to make the beds. The sound of the wind gusting by her windows made Clarie think of last March in Limerock, of hurrying downstreet with the wind pushing her along, and the sun not yet up over the buildings. The gulls would have a rose-gold light on their breasts as they circled high above Main Street.

They had not made her homesick then. No, she was hardly ever homesick after she knew Paul. After she knew Paul, the island stopped being a place to long for, and became a rich treasure which she would share with Paul as soon as summer came.

Summer. The very word was a stab. Would there ever be happy summer again? She fled quickly from it now, down the stairs into the kitchen, putting on a different face. The sister face. But it was wasted because Brian wasn't there, only his empty dishes set tidily on the sink. Anger ran through her like a fire through a dry thicket, all crackling and deadly vigor.

When her mother came into the room Clarie said, "He's run off! I'm not going to stand for it."

"Probably he's gone to the store to get a supply of sour-balls to study on."

Clarie shoved her fists into her pockets before her mother could see them. "No, he's run off. He doesn't intend to study this morning or any morning."

"He's got all day to work in."

"All day to loaf in. I'm going to find him."

"Clarie, wait, *please*," her mother said. "I'll see that he does his work. He can't stay away all day."

"Can't he?" Clarie asked grimly. She knew she couldn't possibly stay in and wait for Brian when she felt like this.

"You know his pride will be touched if his sister comes after him. You might take that into consideration."

"I suppose it's also a matter of pride with him not to do what you want him to," Clarie said. "All right, Mother, I promise we won't come home with a death grip on each other's throats."

She decided to try the fishhouses first. The smoke from their chimneys was shredded into nothing in the stinging brilliant air. Jamie Sorensen, her own age, and his father, Nils, were building traps. They looked at her with identical blue eyes, gave her the same slow warm smiles, and said they hadn't seen him. He wasn't in the Percy fishhouse either, and she knew better than to look in their own. Brian didn't like to work alone at the long and necessary tasks of the lobster fisherman, and some-times gave work to somebody else for an equal amount of work in return.

The wind off the harbor seared the left side of her face, and then she came to the long shed where Charles and Owen Bennett were building a boat. For all Brian growled about the Bennetts, he liked the company of the big dark men. She let herself in and walked through golden shavings.

"Greetings, fair one," Owen Bennett saluted her as she came around the raised hull. "You come to brighten our day?"

"To darken my brother's day if I can lay hands on him."

Owen struck his forehead. "And I was fool enough to think it was me you were after!" Clarie had to laugh in spite of herself. Owen's oldest was twelve, but his black eyes and his laughter were irrepressibly young. She wondered how old you had to be to enjoy life as much as he did.

"Seems like you have a hard time riding herd on that young one," Charles Bennett said. "It's making you old before your time."

"Ayuh, wouldn't it be easier to keep him in a barrel and feed him through the bunghole?" one of the loungers asked, and there was a ripple of laughter. Clar-ie's face was burning. She said coldly, "Well, *has* any-body seen him?"

"I have, missy." A mousy little man spoke up from a checker game. "But you'll have a hard time catching up with him. He went kiting along a half-hour ago or more, with the wind driving him, and his gun under his arm."

"You better go back by the fire and relax, sweetheart," said Owen. "He's long gone."

Charles said kindly, "You'll never keep him at his books on a day like this, or any day, if I know boys. They need some competition, and a few rules to keep 'em in line."

She spun around and went out, kicking up the shavings for want of something better to kick. It was plain to see that they thought of her as a quarrelsome girl always trying to boss a younger brother, who was pretty clever at getting away from her. The heat of her anger warmed her against the wind.

She took the road away from the harbor, along a path the children had tramped bare on their way to and from school. She knew she couldn't catch up with Brian now. There were too many places where he could be safely out of sight, watching for seabirds. But she'd suffocate if she went back home feeling like this, so she kept on walking.

The schoolhouse was a small white building with a belfry, facing out to sea across the deep scallop of School-house Cove. At recess, if no great surf was piling into the cove, the children could play along the beach. Those days for her seemed very long ago, she thought bleakly as she stood on the sea wall and looked down at the calm shimmer of the water.

"Clarie!" The wind brought the voice to her, and she

knew without looking around that the teacher was standing in the schoolhouse doorway. She called again. De-
liberately Clarie jumped off the wall and ran down toward the water until she was sure she was out of sight.
Miss Colwell would think she hadn't heard her, and she
couldn't leave school to call her again. She felt uncomfortable and guilty, but she knew she'd feel worse if she
listened to the teacher saying that Brian was falling back
all the time, that he was losing interest, that—

"Oh, blast them all!" Clarie exploded into the wind,
and tackled the high rocks at the end of the cove. She
followed them around below the Bennett Homestead and
into Goose Cove. From here she climbed up into the
woods to follow the path that led above the deeply in-
dented shore to the southwestern tip of the island.
Chickadees and juncoes flashed about her, sun splashed
through the spruces on her right, and on her left the sea
shone with a gemlike brilliance.

She walked until the woods gave way to steep slopes of
wind-burned turf and scanty snow, and then she went
down into a steep little cove and sat on a log. From here
the surf on the windward side and the wind in the
spruces all blended together in a muted roar like that
heard in a conch shell held to the ear. The cove itself
was utterly silent and calm, burningly bright. And to
Clarie, in this moment, desolate.

She bowed her head onto her knees. *Was* she wrong?
Had she bitten off more than she could chew? But that
question brought her up against the hateful perversity of

Life itself, which could kill her father and allow the violence that Paul had done to her pride and her heart, and now let Brian be hateful and mischievous. "Why can't he do his part," she cried aloud, "when he knows how important that little extra effort is to Mother and me? We're doing *ours!*"

Tears came into her eyes and soaked into the cloth over her knees. She hardly ever cried, and she let herself do it now with self-pity that was very sweet and warming. Well, who's got a better right? she demanded. The trouble was, you couldn't let yourself go on and bawl, your nose always started to run and stopped your breathing. Angrily she fumbled for a handkerchief and found none.

She had heard nothing to warn her that something icy-cold was about to touch her defenseless neck. She straightened up with a gasp, and twisted around to meet the shining amber eyes of a large black dog. It was Peter, Ross Bennett's Labrador, and behind him stood Ross with his gun under his arm, looking down at her.

"What are *you* doing down here?" she snapped, and swung around again, wiping at her face with her sleeve.

"I'm just humoring Pete," said Ross mildly. "I haven't seen a bird, and if I did I wouldn't send him into the water today. But he thinks we're working. What are *you* doing?"

"What's it look like?" She found a handkerchief at last and blew her nose. "Why don't you pretend I'm not here?"

"All right, after you tell me if you're all in one piece.

Haven't broken a leg or something. Haven't just discovered Brian's limp corpse washing around in the rockweed."

"Have you seen him?"

"I saw him on his way to the Eastern End." He sat down on the log beside her. "Mind if I sit long enough to smoke a pipe, if I don't speak to you? Just don't take off as if I was the Headless Man of Damariscove Island. You know, the one who came and sat down alongside a feller and scared him into fits."

It was difficult to say *Don't try to amuse the child* when the Labrador's chin was on her knee. Out of the corner of her eye she couldn't stop watching the man's fingers handling the pipe and tobacco pouch. Her father had smoked a pipe, and Paul was just starting one when it all happened. She'd bought him a special kind of tobacco pouch for his birthday, and it was still hidden away in a corner of her desk drawer. I ought to take it out and burn it, she thought now, or give it to somebody else. Burning it would make Paul too important.

But Paul was still important, her pain told her; she would give almost anything to have him sitting beside her on this log right now. She drifted with a sweet kind of ache into the familiar dream of going to the wharf one boatday and seeing him there on the deck—seeing his face light up with a wonderful incandescence when he saw her. He would leap onto the wharf and reach out for her, saying, "Where can we talk?"

She even had the place chosen, in the woods on the point behind Mark Bennett's house, a warm and se-

31

cluded nook with trees opening on the sea. "I was crazy, I was wrong," Paul would blurt out. "I don't know what ever possessed me, but I want to spend the rest of my life making it up to you. Can you—*will* you—"

She would end it by taking his face in her hands. . . . With a nauseating jolt she was out of the dream, and the eyes that gazed with such adoration into hers belonged to Peter the dog, and beside her Ross was smoking his pipe and looking thoughtfully out to sea.

She got up, pulling down her jacket and zipping it, and Ross handed her up her mittens. "Here. Did I drive you off?"

"No, it's time I went back anyway."

"What's the trouble, Clarie? Life too much for you these days?"

"What do you mean?"

His mouth twitched. "Don't be so ready for a fight. Can't anyone show a friendly interest without your flying at him like a setting hen?"

"I don't like criticism!"

"Who does? And who's criticizing? I meant that this is a pretty dull hard life for you, and there must be times when it weighs mighty heavy on you. You had a good job over there, friends your own age. . . ."

She made her lips tight and started to turn away.

"I saw you once last spring with a blond youngster, floppy forelock, sharp dresser." Ross's unemphatic voice stopped her like a hand on her shoulder. "It was in The Crow's Nest, after the movies one night. You didn't see me, Clarie. You didn't see anybody but him."

32

"So?" She shrugged. "I knew boys over there. Why shouldn't I?" But sickly she saw Paul's face in the soft glow of the lamp in their booth, heard the recorded revival of an old song. *When I grow too old to dream, I'll have you to remember. . . .*

"You do miss him," he said quietly. "Don't you? He wasn't just any boy."

She caught her breath in a sob of hurt and humiliation. "What business is it of yours?" she shouted at his somber face. "And is it anybody's business if Brian and I want to do our father's work? And I'd rather be on this island than anywhere else in the world, and nobody's going to drive me off!"

She left him at a run, racing over the rocks, and didn't look back.

4

THE JANUARY THAW was a promise that spring hadn't really died. There was anguish in it for the Tanners, because last year at this time Ed Tanner had been alive. But still they couldn't help expanding in the gentle air. For Brian and Clarie, to go hauling on these days was a holiday. The seas were fairly calm, and there was no chance of a blizzard setting in between their departure in the morning and their return at night. The island was always to be seen, sometimes shimmering and wavering, rising and falling like an apparition hovering over the sea. Sometimes it was diminished and blue with distance.

Working together out here, they never argued about schoolwork. They left the land behind in more ways than one, and in this fine weather they weren't so obviously watched over, which pleased them both. "Feels good to work without having somebody on your tail all the time," Brian said. "But I suppose Ross will show up when we're hauling the Great Harry, so he can drool a little."

"You act as if that was the only rich spot in these waters," Clarie said. "The Bennetts know places we've never even heard of." She hadn't seen Ross except at a distance since the day they'd met in Chip Cove and she'd tramped off like a spoiled brat—or a hysterical female,

34

she hadn't yet decided which. There was something about him that always brought out the worst in her. But to discover that he knew about Paul—that had been a shocker.

There was no reason for it. Anybody from the island could have run into her with Paul at any time. She hadn't kept him a secret for any wrong purposes, but only because the instant your family or hometown people knew that you liked someone, they looked at you in a different way, asked questions, and either made jokes or were sentimental. The lovely day on which she would introduce Paul and the island to one another had lain ahead of her then. Her father had not yet complained of a headache and lain down and died. But even then, behind her outraged disbelief in this event, there had been the warm knowledge of Paul's love, until she went back to work after that dreadful two weeks and discovered that she had Paul no longer.

The only thing then for which she could be thankful was that no one at home had known about Paul. *But Ross knew.* Why did he have to tell me? she questioned now, desperately. If I just didn't know that *he* knew!

The Great Harry Shoal was responsible for one full crate, as usual. They left its mild disturbance and headed into deep water again. *Sea Dancer* slid down a glistening swell toward the next red and white buoy, and Brian sang, "Come to papa, baby," as the trap rose to the surface. They were moving very slowly, as Clarie watched him opening the trap and reaching inside; then her gaze moved beyond to where a long swell made a peculiar shadow about fifty yards away. Her stomach, lungs, and heart seemed to cramp together in one giant squeeze, because the shadow didn't dissolve in a new swell but moved along intact with a sort of enormous ease. Keeping her eyes on the wet, glistening shape, she reached over and poked Brian. He gave her a startled look, a lobster in his hand, and she shaped the word carefully. *"Whale."*

He looked, opened his mouth, shut it again. Moving very cautiously, he laid the lobster in a crate, then looked again. "What do we do?" Clarie asked close to his ear.

"I can't remember if we just ignore him or try to get invisible."

"He's playing like a porpoise," said Clarie in wonder. "He must like the warm air. Could he be chasing herring this early?"

"I dunno, but he could sink us. How'd you like that tail flapping and slapping around this boat, if he took a notion to come see us?" Brian's own words turned him rather pale. "Cripes, if I slide this trap overboard he'll hear it. Why the devil couldn't you have seen a seal out there?"

"I didn't invent him! Why in heck doesn't he go away?"

"Maybe he thinks this boat is a girl whale," said Brian, "and he's trying to think up a good way to get acquainted."

The whale frolicked massively through the shining swells. Water ran in minature rivers over his sides. He looked larger and closer all the time. Fragments of facts about whales blew like confetti about Clarie's brain, but she couldn't remember anything useful. Brian couldn't stop staring, his hands still gripping the ends of the trap. Clarie looked all around; Joey Caldwell's light-green boat was rocking in the swell off the Seal Rocks, and Charles Bennett's boat was a good distance to the west. And there, just beyond the Great Harry's mild seething, came *Moonlight* at top speed, the bow wave curving away from her on either side like great arched wings.

"There he is, right on schedule!" she cried.

"Hurrying in case he misses something!" After one quick glance Brian was back to watching the whale again. "Hey, it's turning this way, I think!"

Moonlight hit the roughened water around the Great Harry with a wide-open engine. At the noise, the whale sounded. With an immense flirt of its tail, it was gone as if it had never been there, except for a whirlpool of foam and bubbles on the surface. The Tanners still waited. They half-expected that it would appear again, close to them if not actually under *Sea Dancer*.

But nothing happened except that *Moonlight* caught up with them and slowed down to their pace. "Your engine acting up?" Ross called to them. Brian shoved the trap overboard.

"Nope, just watching a whale," he called back.

Ross smiled. "Been watching him quite a while, I'd say. You think he was a man-eater? Moby Dick, maybe?" His dark eyes moved to Clarie.

"He didn't mean us any harm. We could tell."

"Friendly twinkle in the eye, I suppose. Wagging tail. You on your way home?"

"Yep, but we can see the island all nice and clear, Cap'n," said Brian. "I guess we don't need an escort."

"Now that Leviathan's gone, huh?" With a wave Ross turned back to his wheel and speeded up his engine.

"I suppose we could have thanked him for scaring it away," said Clarie, watching the boat go.

"No credit to him. He was checking on us as usual."

"He saw us slowed down a long way off and thought we had engine trouble."

"And wouldn't he like towing us in! Boy, we'd never hear the last of it."

"Are you watching for your next buoy?" she asked crisply.

He gave her a perplexed grin. "Hey—"

"Hay is for horses, better for cows. I wish you'd stop starting every sentence with it. And," she added coldly, staring him down, "there's such a thing as common politeness."

"Is that what's eating you?" His grin became impish. "I thought maybe—"

"Don't think," said Clarie. "*Act*. Gaff that buoy, or is this just a hobby of yours?"

5

THE PARTY at Charles Bennett's wasn't planned. It sprang full-blown from Hugo Bennett's sudden hunger for ice cream. The word went around, and other freezers were put into action, while several women began baking cakes.

When Clarie and her mother came in, around seven, Charles's children had pushed the furniture back against the walls of the long living room, and taken up the rugs. A group of youngsters were doing the Boston Fancy to a rather breathy harmonica tune and the three chords a ten-year-old boy had learned on his older brother Hugo's guitar.

Mrs. Bennett was a small, plump, pretty woman with a slight trace of a French-Canadian accent. Her children ranged from a son away at the Maritime Academy in Castine to the ten-year-old guitar player. Mrs. Owen Bennett was there too, and Owen and Charles were playing chess in the kitchen. The women disappeared to look at some sewing Mrs. Charles was doing, and Clarie sat down where she could watch the prancing children and wish she hadn't come.

Owen pushed back his chair and came over to Clarie, crooking his arm. "Come on, let's show these young ones some real professional style."

She wanted to say no, but he was already pulling her

39

up and drawing her arm through his. The harmonica player was his own Holly, twelve. "Oh Daddy!" she protested in mortification. "Are you going to *dance?*"

"What do you mean, Oh Daddy? I'd be lighter on my feet with rubber boots on than you kids are. You sound like a bunch of horses in here. Strike up some more music."

"I can't. My harmonica's full of spit."

"I'll play for you, Cap'n Owen," said Joey Caldwell from the kitchen, "soon as I shed some clothes." A crowd had arrived at once, and in a few minutes there was a long loud chord on the accordion, and the shout, "Ladies and gentlemen, choose your partners for Lady of the Lake!"

There was a happy scramble as the children and a few adults lined up. The music and the action swept Clarie along. She'd felt leaden and reluctant when Owen had approached her, but her young body had responded in spite of herself. When the dance ended, Ralph Percy and Hugo began a waltz; Ralph was a young red-headed fisherman whose stubby fingers made astonishingly sweet music on a violin, and Hugo at sixteen could almost make a guitar sing by itself.

Jamie Sorensen suddenly stood before Clarie. "Come on," he said. "I'll be darned if I dance with a twelve-year-old kid or one of my aunts."

Out in the kitchen cribbage and checkers went on, and a great deal of visiting. The party was well under way, and Clarie had no time to think hard or deep. Boys were sent to the well several times for fresh drinking water,

40

and the children grew more exhilarated as the evening went on. The smaller ones were bedded down around the house; a few older ones, wild with excitement, went out to play hide-and-seek. Clarie, going to the pantry for a drink, stood watching the slim figures leaping from rock to rock in the bright moonlight above the shimmering cove. She remembered with envy the ecstasy of such occasions. When these children were very old they would say to their great-grandchildren, "I remember playing out of doors in winter, late at night, and the moon was so bright you could see colors, and there was no wind. . . . You could hear the music in the house, and see the people dancing by the windows."

"Lonesome for somebody, Clarie?" a soft voice said behind her. It was Ralph's wife Marjorie. She was a mainland girl who had happily become an islander.

"No, I'm just watching the kids and wishing I was kid enough to be out there with them."

"I know what you mean. Whenever I see a perfect place in the woods for a playhouse I wish I was about ten again." She took a glass of water. "But you must have enjoyed working for the Ryders. They're nice people, I think."

"Yes, they are," Clarie said. She felt a warning chill between her shoulder blades. But Marjorie didn't mention Paul. She said, "Do you ever miss the shop? Maybe that's a silly question, because I certainly didn't miss my job."

"I don't know if I miss it, but I think of it sometimes, and the Ryders." Just in case Marjorie had an idea she was too tactful to express, she added, "When I was little I wanted to grow up to be a lobsterman so I'd never have to leave the island. I didn't see why a girl couldn't earn her living that way."

Ralph poked his red head in. "Oh, here's my little wifie! Let's see, which do I want for Hull's Victory? Eeny-meenie miney-mo—"

"I'm out anyway," protested Marjorie, "because I can't do Hull's Victory. It's too darned involved. Who *was* Hull, anyway?"

"I should never have married an intellectual," said Ralph, dragging Clarie out behind him. Clarie reflected that the plainest girl in the world would be a belle on Bennett's Island if she could dance.

Now the women began setting out dishes, the cakes were cut, and the boys went out to remove the swathings of old burlap bags from the freezers. The scattered children gathered as if summoned by a magic signal.

The ice cream was old-fashioned vanilla, rich and yellow. The silence of satisfaction settled over the house. Clarie took her dish into the front hall and sat on the stairs with a clutch of little girls ranging from six years to Linnie Sorensen's fourteen. There were times when children were the safest company. They asked the least pointed questions and offered no advice.

Hugo Bennett wandered out after a while with his guitar, and Brian and Matt Fennell came with him. His first chords brought more people out into the hall, and the singing began. The songs were western, southern,

42

popular, and the old standbys which drew the parents in. Soon a nostalgic mood possessed everyone as they sang. Clarie let herself go as she had gone with the dancing, in a web spun of deep voices and light ones. A child's absorbed face by lamplight as he sang with all his might; Hugo's black head bent over the guitar; her mother smiling faintly as she listened; the teacher looking pretty and young, singing *Loch Lomond* with a small child in her lap. Ross Bennett was standing behind her. He must have come in late; Clarie realized she hadn't seen him all evening.

"But me and my true love will never meet again. . . ."

Ross was looking straight at her across the others, and she was ridiculously embarrassed. She turned her head away and leaned it against the wall, tired and depressed all at once. She didn't know who suggested it, but now they were starting *When I Grow Too Old To Dream.*

"Don't you know this one?" Linnie said in her ear. "It's awful old but it's real pretty. Daddy said it came out when he was going around with Mama."

"I can't sing any more," said Clarie, "I'm getting hoarse." There was no way to escape without being conspicuous, so she sat quiet, trying to look merely reflective. The party was beginning to break up. Some islanders had already gone, and Mrs. Owen Bennett was crooking a finger at her two while they tried to ignore her.

Now the singing was really over, and there was a good-natured confusion of conversation. Clarie had left her things in the girls' room, and when she returned to the kitchen someone told her that her mother had gone with

the older Sorensens.   Glad of a chance to be alone for a
little while in the moonlight, she thanked Mrs. Charles
for a nice evening and slipped around Owen and Laurie,
who were each bundling a child into a coat.   Out in the
windless cold a group of boys stood by the corner of the
house, hands in pockets and shoulders hunched.   They
were Brian, Jamie, Hugo, and Matt Fennell.

"Hey, let's walk Clarie home," Matt suggested boldly.
He was all of fourteen.   Jamie clapped him on the
shoulder and stepped away from the rest.

"You're all too late.   What do you think I've been
waiting for?"   He took her elbow, and she resisted in-
stinctively.   Then, glancing into his face, she saw his
quiet smile and the odd deep sparks of moonlight reflected in his eyes.   His hair looked almost white-blond.
Paul's hair had been a darker color, and grew differ-
ently. . . .   Why not go with Jamie? she thought suddenly.   I've been forgetting there are other men in the
world.

They left in a shower of juvenile comment, advice, and
whistles, and were halfway down the field when Hugo's
voice carried distinctly above the rest.   "Wait up, Ross,
and give the young lovers a chance to get away."

"You want to go straight home, or take a walk first?"
Jamie asked Clarie.   "It's a pretty night.   Weather-
breeder."

She found it difficult to reply when she felt so unreal.
This was like walking in a dream, companioned by
someone whom you knew in real life but never expected

44

to meet in a dream. Sometimes this happened, and the next day you looked at that person with different eyes, either with amusement, interest, or embarrassment. How would she look at Jamie tomorrow? she wondered. The experience could be—what?

"Intriguing?" she murmured.

"Who, me?"

They laughed, but she was already seeing him with different eyes. It was a familiar joke that any girl who was interested in Jamie would have to make all the advances, but he hadn't done too badly tonight. "Let's go out on Eastern Harbor Point," she suggested.

They went very quietly along the boardwalk laid over the rough ground between the houses on this side of the harbor and their wharves and fishhouses.

Past the last house now they climbed a slope frosty with moonlight and splashed with the jet shadows of spruces. The harbor was on their left, the boats gleaming white on motionless water that was neither black nor blue but a subtle blend of the two. Sometimes a windshield flashed a reflection of the moon. Clarie felt like drifting without words or thoughts in the dreamlike atmosphere.

Behind her Jamie said huskily, "Clarie, if you—what I mean is, if you're of a mind to go around with me, I'd like it fine." He slid his arms around her, gently at first, and then tightening the embrace, and put his cheek against her hair. "I've been wanting to say it for a long time, but you always looked so darn stern."

Her heart was beating with unnecessary speed, seeing

45

that she wasn't in love with Jamie. But there was something—well, *pleasant* about the whole thing. It had been a long time.... Still gazing at the harbor, she said, "Then I must have looked different tonight."

"You did," he said. "You *do*. Up there dancing, and now, in the moonlight."

"How do I look different?"

"Pretty." He got the word out with an effort, and then after a tense moment he said, "Mysterious."

She wanted to laugh, not at him but perhaps at the irony of the fact that she looked pretty and mysterious to the wrong person. She heard Paul's voice in her head like a counterpoint to Jamie's. *I'm sorry, Clarie, but I can't help myself. I don't know what there is about her.*

She had to stop that tune from playing. She put her hands down on Jamie's and broke his grip, and turned to face him in the circle of his arms. In the moonlight he too was mysterious, his eyes not blue but dark, his face not the youthful one she had known but that of a man she had never seen before. She put her hands on his shoulders.

"Let's not rush anything, Jamie," she said. "Tonight I—I just don't know."

"Sure, Clarie. Sure." He leaned toward her and she let his lips brush hers before she moved her head away. It wasn't a dream after all. Dreams swept you on, for good or ill, and in some fantastic way all the decisions were made for you.

"I guess I'd better go home, Jamie," she said.

"Will you go for a walk with me down around Sou-west Point the next good day that we don't have to haul?" he asked.

She started to laugh. "As one good lobsterman to another, we ought to have plenty to talk about. Like 'is bream better than salt herring to catch lobsters? Do you prefer your baitbags dipped in preservative,' or 'do you use nylon twine?' Or—"

He wrapped her in his arms and gave her a hard hug. "I guess we could find something else besides business to talk about."

"I knew a boy over in Limerock who used to take his girl out to the dump to shoot rats. They liked it better than going to the movies."

He nuzzled his face into her hair. "Gorry, too bad we don't have a dump. Or rats. But we could shoot at somebody's pot buoys."

"Yes, we could. And now I'm going home."

He kept one arm around her until they reached the boardwalk and had to go single file; he didn't offer to kiss her at the door, and she felt a surge of affection toward him for that. She needed time to move from the world of Paul into the possible world of Jamie, and she was so tired of feeling hurt and alone that she found herself longing for the change.

47

6

THE STORM CAME—two days of snow and rain and sleet that left the island looking drenched enough to be picked up and wrung out. But the winds were gentle, and on the first good day to haul after the storm, Clarie was ready to go by the time the sunrise was turning the eastern sky to apricot-gold. Brian had not yet come downstairs.

"I'm going up and get him," she said. "I spoke to him an hour ago, on my way down."

"Did he answer?"

"He made a sound like Hodge when he thinks you want his mouse."

Margaret Tanner laughed. "Very descriptive. . . . Clarie, did it ever occur to you that something may be catching up with him?"

"Like what?"

"Well—fatigue, I guess. You two have been making a terrific effort for a long time, and—"

"I'll say it's terrific! We've been doing darn well, everybody says so. Of course it's been a good open winter and that's a help," she conceded.

"But it's a long hard business," said her mother, "and Brian's still growing. The strain could be catching up with him, you know."

"Mother, we haven't been out for three days. He

should be good and rested. I am. I can hardly wait to get out there and see how many traps we've lost, and how many have shifted, and—"

"Sometimes as long as you keep going you can ignore things, but if you let up they come at you all at once, and then it's hard to get going again. Awfully hard." She turned around to the dresser and Clarie looked guiltily at her back. Her mother could be speaking of her own experience.

"Well, anyway," she said gruffly, "it strikes me mighty peculiar that he only gets so tired when it's anything to do with work."

"Miss Colwell and I had a talk up at the Bennetts' the other night. She says it's boring for most youngsters to work alone, and difficult too, without a schedule of some sort to hold them in line." She fastened the cover of a lunch box. "He's not really behind now—not so far behind that a couple of weeks wouldn't bring him up." She fastened the other lunch box. "If he started school on the mainland before too long he could be with his class. If he continues to go behind, he may lose a whole year."

Clarie felt stunned. She had been almost happy when she got up. Paul had seemed very far off, even if Jamie seemed no closer to her. "Mother, you never used to be so weak!" she burst out. "Brian's only fifteen, you can tell him what to do and expect to be obeyed, but you're acting as if there's nothing you can do about it if he won't study."

"You know I keep him at it as much as possible," her

mother's low controlled voice went on. "But he's fidgety and can't concentrate for long. Part of the reason is the upset in all our lives, and another part is that he's not living a natural life for a boy his age. He should be working *or* in school, not both."

"We've done a good job for five months, and we can keep on, if he'd stop appealing for sympathy. He can't fool me, Mother, I'm too close to him."

"Maybe you *are* too close to him, dear," said her mother. "And maybe you're protesting too much about yourself. It could be getting too much for you."

"*Me?*" Clarie gasped. "I *love* this life! I wouldn't want any other kind!" To give up? To live on the mainland where Paul had hurt and humiliated her?

Her mother said after a moment, "I see," and Clarie hoped she saw what she was intended to see. "Maybe you'd better call Brian after all. It looks like a fine day out."

"You call him, Mother, will you? I'll go down and bring the boat in. I hardly ever get a chance to, Brian's so crazy about that engine. . . . You know what, I'll bet if he thought he might get lugged off the island to go to school he'd really buckle down to his books."

Her mother smiled. "Maybe. All right, go along. Just be careful where it's frosty and icy. I warn you, Clarie, a broken leg would take all three of us off the island quicker than anything."

Clarie grinned. "Four of us. Don't forget Hodge." She felt good again when she got outside into the crystal-line air that tingled in her throat and nostrils. Another shoal spot safely passed, within the sound of breakers. That meant a spell of security for a while, until something threw them off course again.

She crossed the iron-hard road to the Tanner fishhouse and went down onto the tiny patch of sand between their wharf and the Percies'. Their skiff was tied up high and dry and she was working at the frozen knot when somebody spoke from up above. "Can you make it or do you need a knife?"

She looked up and saw Ross Bennett on the wharf. "Hi," she said, and went back to working on the knot. "No, thanks, I can get it. There, it's loosened."

He came down the ladder at the side of the wharf, turned the skiff over, and slid it down to the water, all with a quiet, almost indifferent, expression.

"Thank you very much," said Clarie stiffly. "I wasn't expecting any assistance. Anyway, I thought everybody else had gone."

"I'm late this morning."

"We are too. Brian overslept."

A crinkle of humor appeared around his eyes. "You going to haul the gear all alone?"

"Nope, but I get a chance to start the engine for a change." She stepped into the bow of the skiff and over the middle seat to reach the stern, and thus float the skiff off, but she didn't place her foot firmly enough and it shot along the frost-slick bottom; there was an instant of frantic struggle during which her mother's words shot sickeningly through her.... "A broken leg ..." Then it was over and she was sprawled over the middle seat

51

with no wind and her pulse-beat roaring in her ears. Shock had blasted away self-consciousness; she gazed helplessly into Ross Bennett's face as he bent over her. Not having any breath she couldn't tell him anything, but gravely he took one ankle and then the other and straightened out her legs. She moved her feet and knees and was reassured.

"Good thing you didn't go overboard," Ross said dryly. "Anybody could get real wet like that. Ready to stand up?"

"Yes," she wheezed. Getting her wind back was exquisite agony. He half-lifted her and she pushed with her hands till she was sitting on the seat.

"You want to go back ashore and rest up?"

She shook her head. "No, I'm all right," she breathed. "In a minute. . . . Long as I didn't break anything." She began to be humiliated about her tumble. "Would you give me a little shove off, please? And thank you very much for helping me up. I guess I'd still be sitting there wondering what happened." He gave her the push, and when she got the skiff turned around bow first, she saw him going back up the ladder again and then leaving the wharf.

Darn him, she thought hotly, I must have looked a complete idiot, stepping into that skiff like Airy-Fairy Lillian and landing on the back of my neck.

Brian was on the wharf as she maneuvered *Sea Dancer* alongside the end where the water was deep. She shut off the engine. "How was that? She brushed the spilings soft as a baby's kiss."

Brian said sourly, "You were in so much of a hurry you didn't lug anything down. I had oilclothes, lunches, everything."

"Oh, poor boy. I suppose that exhausted you so that you couldn't manage to get the bait out."

"I *have* got the bait out," said Brian with dignity, and pitched a bundle of oilclothes at her. She fought her way free of a jacket that fell over her head and gave him a saccharine smile. "Temper, brother dear."

Not speaking they lowered the baskets of herring-stuffed baitbags aboard by the hoist. It would be a good day but a silent one, she thought, as Brian took the wheel still without a word in her direction. She wondered if their mother had been talking to him or if he was just cranky from being roused and rushed.

Well, I'm cranky, too, she thought, and it started out to be such a wonderful day.

They made the run to the west still without speaking. Their first string of twenty-five traps had been shifted by the storm, but the buoys were clearly in view on the vast, gently-heaving slopes of water. Later, three traps were missing, evidently swept toward a ledge and pounded to pieces on the rocks. They saw one of their buoys gleaming in the drifts of fresh rockweed flung up high on the ledge, but they had no skiff with them so they had to leave it.

At the Great Harry Shoal, the swell left over from the storm caused the usual turbulence, and two of their traps had moved together so that their warps were entangled. It took both Clarie and Brian to clear the snarl and get

53

the traps hauled. Their arms were tired at the end—at least Clarie's were, and she knew that Brian felt it even though he wouldn't admit it. But as usual they left the Great Harry with an almost-full crate on the stern, alongside the one they had already filled.

Clarie poured out more cocoa into her thermos cup and sipped it as she steered. When she glanced around at Brian he was sitting on the engine box, staring at the platform between his boots. What if he *were* as tired as their mother had suggested? Oh, he *isn't!* she answered herself in irritation. He just feels silent this morning. Anybody has a right to be silent. It's the only way you can be alone sometimes.

The Sorensen boat was off to the north, Jamie and his father hauling together. What was Jamie really like? She'd known him for all her life on Bennett's Island, gone through each grade with him at school, graduated from Limerock High in the same class with him. But to know anyone like this wasn't to know him at all on the deeper level of intimacy known as "going around together."

"*Hey!*" Brian dug her in the ribs, and she jumped, expecting to see the whale again, surfacing across their bows. Instead, one of their buoys was swimming past. She swung the wheel down hard to take the boat in a wide arc, and Brian grinned at her maliciously.

She brought *Sea Dancer* up neatly beside the buoy and Brian gaffed it. While he was brushing the sea urchins and starfish off the wet laths he glanced around, raised his

54

eyebrows, and said, "Where is our guardian angel, chaperon, Gestapo agent?"

"Didn't you see him in the harbor? He hadn't left when we did. Maybe he didn't get out at all."

"Broke down, I hope," said Brian. "Funny how crowded he can make the ocean."

"That whale made it seem pretty crowded the other day too." Clarie squinted nervously at a long shadow that formed as a sea rolled up. The shadow dissolved.

"I wasn't scared," Brian said. "I was just afraid he'd damage the boat."

"And leave us overboard in January," said Clarie. "I suppose we could have sat on the lobster crates and paddled five miles home with our hands."

Brian laughed. The day's ice was broken at last. "Well, after all, some doryman rowed miles and miles with his hands frozen to the oars. I sh'd think we could go riding home like a fly on a mussel shell."

Clarie looked around to spot their next buoy, and discovered signs of trouble. Two other lobstermen also had traps in this vicinity, and here there had been some shifting of gear in the storm. A black and yellow buoy was floating close to a red and white Tanner buoy, a striped blue and orange one knocked clumsily against the black and yellow.

"Look at that snarl," she called to Brian. "Foss Campion and Joey Caldwell are right on top of us!"

"Now that's a pretty sight," he said in disgust.

"Let's leave it for Foss and Joey to take care of," said

55

Clarie. Even though the men had gone out earlier, they went farther for their deeper-set traps, and would haul along here on their way home.

"I'm going to haul that trap, chum," Brian said. "We're out here and there's nobody riding herd on us for once, and I'm not leaving one trap unhauled."

"Look, I can still remember how my hands and arms ached when we cleared that little snarl. Let's go around it."

Brian shoved the trap overboard and gave her a steely glare. "In a pig's eye. Look, if one or the other of 'em, or both together, get working on that snarl and something has to be cut, whose trap will they cut off first?"

"You don't know that they'd cut off ours. Anyway, we haven't lost a trap yet from anybody cutting them off in a snarl, so I don't know why you're getting so worried all of a sudden."

"Come on, give her some gas," he said irritably.

She speeded up the engine and headed toward the snarl. He would soon find out that they couldn't clear it and be willing to leave it for the men.

He started off calmly enough, with a great air of efficiency, giving her orders with which she didn't argue. But a tangle of three buoys floating at the end of forty-five fathoms of rope from three water-soaked, rock-ballasted lobster traps, was not to be easily managed. Between the futile effort, the cold air, the wet ropes, Clarie's fingers began to lose power. Brian's face was flushed and his motions became fast and jerky, as if he thought that by sheer violence he could spin the twisted warps apart

56

and slat the heavy traps across the bottom like so many dry chips.

Clarie let a nylon warp slide out of her hands and began trying to wring feeling into her fingers.

"Come on," she said to Brian as he hung over the side, muttering and pulling. "Let's leave it."

He gave her a look brilliant with fury. "I'm not leaving that trap!" He reached back to the engine box, to the square cookie tin holding a few trap nails, a hammer, and some short lengths of traphead twine for doing any small mending jobs that might come up as they hauled. His knife lay open in the box.

"Hey!" Clarie protested. "Who are you going to cut?"

"Not us, sister." He gave her a tense grin.

She got the knife before he did. "You're not going to cut off anybody else! If you weren't so tired and ugly you wouldn't be so foolish!"

"Who's foolish?" He was pale around the mouth.

"You are! Now throw those buoys overboard and let's get back to work."

"I will not throw them overboard!"

"Then I'll heave your knife." It was one of his greatest treasures, a gift from his father.

"If you do—"

"If I do, *what?*" They tried to stare each other down, and suddenly Brian's eyes glittered with a rush of tears. He turned quickly and began tossing the buoys over the side, shoving off the Campion trap that they'd been able to haul up onto the washboard. She pitied him for having to surrender, but she knew she was right.

57

They had been rocking gently without power, and she started up the engine and headed for the next buoy. They hauled through the rest of the string without speaking. Then they were done and on the way home, two full crates loaded on the stern and one in the cockpit with them. Brian was steering, aloof in his secret thoughts. Clarie poured out some cocoa and held the cup under his nose.

"Have some quick energy," she invited. He pulled back.

"Oh, come down off your high horse," she teased him. "You know you wouldn't really have cut off those traps."

"Yes, I would, and I wish they'd been Ross Bennett's."

"Leave Ross out of this. He's never done anything to you."

"What are you sticking up for him for?"

"Watch your wheel, sonny," she said. "They hadn't moved the Ripper last time I knew."

"We're nowhere near the Ripper." But he glanced involuntarily ahead and to port; a long low curling breaker seemed to rise out of nowhere. It dissolved in foam and disappeared and then everything looked as before. "And Foss and Joey are set too close to us, anyway."

"Oh, they are not! It was the storm that did it." She laughed at him, waiting for him to respond, but when the change didn't come she was angry. "Stop sulking and grow up. At least you can let people *think* you're not an irresponsible kid."

58

His cheeks flamed. "Oh, dry up! You're always prodding me and chewing at me about something. Who in heck do you think you are? The heir-apparent or something?"

Now her face went on fire. "What do you mean by *that?*"

"You know what I mean!" he shouted. "You act as if you had to do all the thinking and planning for this family or we'd just fold up and melt away without you to breathe for us!"

"And *you* act as if you'd never learned a thing from Father or from anybody else! At home you're leaning on your oars instead of doing your schoolwork, and out here you act like this spoiled kid who's going to go slatting and slamming through everything with your big boat and your knife, and—"

Brian slapped her face, and she slapped him back. "Now who's acting like a spoiled kid!" he taunted her, laughing with excitement. She didn't answer, she was too busy trying to grab him and shake him. Brian kept on laughing and dodging, holding her off.

"No place for a girl out here anyway!" he told her. "You're going all to pieces just because you can't do everything yourself, haul and bait, measure lobsters and plug 'em, and steer, and take the money, and stand around the car!" She caught hold of his oilskin sleeve, but he moved swiftly and grabbed her wrists. "Hey, Clarie, you could bait up if you wanted to. I've been paying Ronnie and Tod, but you could do it for nothing! Jamie'd be crazy about the perfume!"

59

"That's it!" she flared at him. "That's the end! I'm through! I'm through with everything!"

As she cried out the passionate words the boat lifted under them with a slow yet dreadful steadiness. They were both struck rigid, their staring eyes transmitting messages of warning and fear. The upward motion seemed to go on forever, the engine could not make them outrun whatever massive force it was that lifted them. *The whale!* Clarie thought.

But Brian pointed, his mouth open as if he couldn't breathe. They were being carried upward and forward on a rising, curling sea; while they had squabbled, and forgotten the wheel, *Sea Dancer* had changed her course, and the strong-running tide had pulled her toward the sea-hidden ledge called the Ripper. They stood waiting for the sea to break under them, for the boat to drop, for the ledge to show black and lethal through the foam. *Get the life jackets!* Clarie wanted to shout. But she couldn't speak. "I'm through with everything!" she had said, and now when the sea broke and the bottom of the boat dropped and shattered on the rocks, they would all be through with everything; she and Brian and *Sea Dancer*.

Brian was staring hard over the side. Suddenly his hand moved and *Sea Dancer* lunged forward, rolled, righted herself, rolled down the other way, tossed about like a toy boat in a tide pool made stormy by a child's stick. But no splintering jar happened under Clarie's feet, and just aft of the stern the comber had broken into swirling foam. A black point of ledge showed for an instant like a shark's fin. They had outrun the danger and were now thrown about in the deep swell surrounding the Ripper. Brian was also watching the action astern; their eyes met, too scared yet to smile, and ashamed. Then, as they rolled deeply again, a startled expression shot across his face, and she looked aft in time to see one of their full crates slide overboard off the stern, and start to bob away from them rapidly in the confused currents, about to be sucked back into the danger they had just passed. She had no thought, she simply moved. She was flat on her stomach across the stern, reaching hard with the long gaff. The hook caught in the rope loop at one end of the crate in the last possible instant.

She knew Brian couldn't come and help her yet. He had to take the *Sea Dancer* a safe distance away from the turbulence, so she lay there praying that her grip and her shoulder would hold out against the pull of a hundred-pound crate of lobsters. She had to hold onto the stern bit with the other hand to keep from being pulled overboard herself. She could feel her slippery oilclothes sliding a little on the wet wood and thought, Maybe the crate isn't worth it, but just a little more—

Suddenly the boat was in comparatively calm water and the strain abruptly ceased. Brian appeared beside her, and together they pulled the crate in, and back aboard. Panting, dry-mouthed, they peeled off their soaked gloves. Brian went back to the wheel and she opened a lunch box. "How about some soul-and-body lashin'?" she asked him with a weak grin.

"Ayuh! Got anything left to drink?"

61

"Plenty." She filled two cups from the thermos and passed him one. As he took it she said, "No more fights."

"Not aboard the boat, anyway. Let's slug it out on solid ground." Their laughter came then, exhilarated, drunken. They were alive, and they'd saved the crate of lobsters.

"You opened her up at just the right moment," she said. "How'd you know when?"

"I didn't." He wasn't bragging now. He was a puzzled, thankful, and wondering boy. "I don't even remember thinking."

"That means good reflexes," she complimented him.

"You've got some pretty good ones yourself, the way you dived for that crate."

"Thanks." They drank their cocoa, eyes on the way ahead. The course for home lay fair and blue in the rich gold light of mid-afternoon. The island slopes were a warm tawny color between the two blues of spruce woods and ocean.

"Good thing Captain Bligh never caught up with us today," said Brian. "He'd have been torn between his better impulses and letting us drown."

"And if we survived he'd go back and get up a petition to take us off the water as a menace to ourselves and navigation." While Brian appreciated this, Clarie thought back to the morning. Between her tumble in the skiff and her scramble after the crate she was going to have a few bruises. . . . It would have been rather wonderful to see *Moonlight* riding close by about the time she was braced for the ghastly crunching of timbers under her feet. She looked astern involuntarily and saw Joey's boat beyond the Great Harry, and Charles Bennett going toward the Seal Rocks.

"You going to tell anybody about this?" Brian asked her suddenly. "I mean, the whale was one thing, everybody tells about seeing whales, but—"

"You mean admit that we were a couple of farmers out here, sailing square over the Ripper?"

"*Square*'s the right word," said Brian. "Two of them."

"I don't even want to remember this myself," said Clarie, "let alone share it with anybody as a priceless gem."

7

A s IF the nearly fatal experience aboard the boat had worked as a sort of catharsis, there was a change in both Brian and Clarie. That night Brian got out his books without prompting, and again the next morning. He worked, not as if he actually enjoyed it, but as if he had made up his mind to pitch into an essential job and do it as well as possible.

As for Clarie, she had a lame knee and a stiff shoulder to remind her that life, even without Paul, could be very sweet. It was ungrateful to God to kick and sulk and complain, when they'd escaped the Ripper. For death it would have been, even with life jackets, if they had stayed more than ten minutes in that icy water.

Armored in this knowledge, she was ready to go for a walk with Jamie when he came for her. He had a sheathed hatchet hanging from his belt, and was going to cut pot limbs. "It's a real saving, you know that?" he said as they struck out for Goose Cove. "I figured up what I saved last year by making my own bows and funny-eyes instead of buying them." The bows were the arches onto which the laths were nailed to make the lobster traps. The funny-eyes were the small hoops that held the trapheads open to make an entrance for lobsters.

"I don't think that spruce funny-eyes hold up in nylon heads the way the metal ones do," argued Clarie. They stopped to watch a black duck family take off from the surface of the cove. "And besides, I like the brass-colored ones because they're prettier. The last heads Brian and I knit were that pale blue twine that Mark had, and those heads were just beautiful. They looked almost like lace, and with those shiny gold rings they were too handsome to put into traps and sink out of sight."

Jamie began to laugh. "I thought for a minute there we were talking like one lobsterman to another, the way you said we would, but by gorry, you're a girl after all."

She had to laugh too. If there'd been any self-consciousness between them it was gone now. It was good to have someone to walk with on Bennett's Island on a fine afternoon. "Spruce gum!" she said avidly, trying to pry the aromatic amber gob off the tree trunk.

"Wait a minute, I'll get it," Jamie said. "Awful stuff. But we pounce on it like fish hawks on a school of herring."

"We're fixated because when we were kids we went over this island like a swarm of locusts, eating everything we could get our hands on, so now we're fixated. Spruce gum, fern roots—"

"Those new little green spruce tips." Jamie's eyes gleamed. "Young raspberry leaves. Sorrel. Bunchberries, raspberries, blackberries, field strawberries."

"Green apples! My mouth's puckering up now."

"Talk about puckering up your tonsils, how about chewing raw cranberries?" He spoke through thrashing boughs as he cut off a half-dozen suitable ones. "Dry fish. Remember the time I salted and dried all those

65

harbor pollock I caught? I spent so much time trying to keep the flies off 'em I couldn't look a dry fish in the eye for as much as a year afterward."

At Sou-West Point they sat on a hillside overlooking the endless play of surf, and ate apples and chocolate bars. Then they began beachcombing their way back. The shores at this end of the island were rich in plunder. They found some new planks in the rockweed, and a brand-new lobster crate with no name burned into it; and several traps—identified by their buoys—that had come ashore intact during the storm. The wreckage of a skiff told its own story. One sturdy varnished oar was ensnared in rockweed, and they looked for the mate but couldn't find it. They dragged everything worth saving well above the tide line. When they reached the woods Clarie helped to carry the rope-tied bundles of boughs left here and there along the path. She stopped once, held an aromatic green armful before her face, and intoned:

"Fear not, 'Till Birnam Wood remove to Dunsinane.' "

Jamie groaned. "Don't bring up those days to spoil a perfectly good afternoon."

" 'Double, double toil and trouble,' " she snarled. " 'Fire burn and cauldron bubble.' "

"Can we talk about something else more fascinating to me personally?"

"What, for instance?" She rearranged her load. "I know why you asked me along today. To help you lug your stuff."

"Ayuh, and you're supposed to walk ten paces behind

66

me, all bowed down with your burdens." He stood in her way. "I want to talk about you," he said gruffly. Color swept up his face as rapidly as dismay swept over her. "Have you done any thinking yet? You know anything yet?" The color deepened. She thought desperately, Most girls would know how to turn this off, or to go along with it without committing themselves. But I'm not most girls. . . .

"I know I've had a good time this afternoon," she said at last. "I don't know anything else yet. Jamie, things don't happen to me like—like lightning striking!" It did with Paul, but she'd never let it be so again. "Old Slow but Sure, that's me." She tried to laugh. He dropped his branches and put his hands on either side of her waist. They were big and very strong, holding her fast. His eyes went over her face, narrowing slightly as if he were searching unknown waters for a marker to show his course.

"I'll have to be satisfied with that," he said at last. "What gowels me is all the time I've wasted. You've been home here since last summer, and I've been treating you like one of the boys."

Suddenly he pulled her to him and kissed her hard and quick, then held her off to look at her.

She said unhappily, "I don't want to keep you dangling."

"I'll take my chances," he said.

They collected their bundles and went down out of the woods and across Goose Cove Beach. School was out, and from up around the Bennett Homestead the shouts of children carried in the gray quiet air. They cut across the meadow toward the woods which lay behind the Sorensen house.

"Listen," said Clarie, and they stopped to hear the small sharp voices of nuthatches and the sociable whistles of chickadees. The bell-like call of a blue jay rang from farther off in the woods, and there was a sudden raucous, disorderly clatter of crows.

Clarie leaned against a thick birch trunk and watched the acrobatics of chickadees overhead, then let her glance slide sideways, to see Jamie without his noticing.

What was he? A good lobsterman at nineteen, with his own large string of traps, his own boat, though he and his father doubled up in winter. An islander, even more so than herself, because his parents had been born there, and his mother was a Bennett. He'd been brought up by a father who was one of the most respected men on the island. It was almost certain that Jamie would be the same sort of man. These were the things you were supposed to consider, but who did?

No, you went by the unpredictable events, what happened to your stomach and your heartbeat at the sound of a voice and the most casual touch of a hand. You went by what jumped into your mind before you woke up in the morning, what drifted through it at the edge of sleep at night, and by the way you were tightened to a fine pitch all day, waiting for the expected—or unexpected—encounter.

She'd known it all with Paul, and a longing sharp as pain pierced the moment. Yet, even in that intolerable instant, she wondered for the first time whether it was Paul for whom she longed, or what had gone with him.

"Clarie," Jamie said in a low voice. She braced herself to meet his somber blue eyes. "My mother made mince-meat turnovers this morning," he told her, "and I'm standing here quietly starving to death."

She began to laugh, and then they went along through the birches.

8

THE NEXT good work day spit freezing rain at times and showed uncertain sunshine at others, and always kept the boat tossing and bouncing. The Tanners jogged toward home in mid-afternoon. Brian stood at the wheel, apparently absorbed in his own thoughts. Yet his eyes constantly swept the water ahead, as Clarie's did, for buoys, floating logs, and anything else that shouldn't be there.

Brian had grown in one respect since they started lobstering. His idea used to be to run the engine at full speed always, when not hauling; never to humor the boat, but to smash through seas regardless of wind and tide. Now he eased along at a respectable speed, taking account of the contrary directions of the breeze and the current. Though once in a while he gave in to the impulse to "let 'er rip," he had begun to consider both boat and engine as precious properties to be taken care of.

As usual no one else was going home at the same time, and for the last few times they'd hauled, Ross Bennett hadn't caught up with them near the Great Harry Shoal. Clarie had seen him in the store and around the harbor, at which time her bruises seemed to come burningly to life as if they'd shoot flame through her clothes.

Brian always looked ostentatiously for Ross when they approached the Great Harry, and had something to say at

70

which she laughed. But just the same, she wondered about Ross. Not that it mattered, she mused now as *Sea Dancer* jogged across the choppy white-streaked water. He probably thinks we're not worth worrying about.

She shrugged as if someone had challenged her in an argument and she couldn't think of a good answer.... He's odd. Not like the rest of the Bennetts. He never has much to say, but then that time he tried to talk to me in Chip Cove I wasn't very encouraging.... She blushed at the memory of the way she'd flown at him.... A good thing he's the silent kind, she added cynically, or he'd have spread that about Paul and me all over the place. I suppose I owe him thanks because nobody knows I had a man who walked out on me when I went home to my father's funeral....

Brian called to her and she looked where he was pointing. "Cap'n Owen's broken down, it looks like."

White Lady was drifting, they could tell by her aimless progress. "I hope it's only engine trouble," Clarie said. No Bennett's Islander had ever yet disappeared from his boat while hauling, but it had happened to other fishermen sometimes. A pot warp could make a "riding turn" around a leg or wrist and drag a man overboard and down with the trap to drown, or he might have a heart attack, a stroke, or a freak skid on a slippery deck.

"He's probably sitting down smoking and swearing," said Brian. "She started acting up outside, most likely, and he headed home and she flunked out again. He's letting her drift to get as near land as possible, but if he can't get her going pretty soon he'll have to anchor."

Brian was already turning *Sea Dancer* to the east. "I'll bet he's doing some plain and fancy cussing!"

As they got closer, they could see Owen sitting on the washboard, his big shoulders hunched over. Brian slowed down and they jogged alongside. Clarie's stomach lurched suddenly. He was scowling furiously at the piece of rope he had twisted around his upper left arm, and kept twisting tight with his right hand. His left hand was held up, the fingers splayed out as if helpless, and the hand was red with blood. It had soaked the cuff of his gray and green flannel shirt, and was running in red streams down the arm of his yellow oiljacket.

"Can either of you two," Owen growled without looking at them, "fix this blasted tourniquet?"

One glance at Brian's face told Clarie he wasn't the one. She stepped across onto *White Lady*'s washboard and jumped down. Her teeth were set hard. Why couldn't it have been somebody else who saw him? she thought. But nobody else had, and there was nothing to be done but help him as much as she could. Her scarf was already in her hand and as she approached him he let go the piece of rope.

"I can't hold it tight enough long enough," he explained. Sweat ran down his face. She tied the scarf around his arm, wishing there was some way to get his oiljacket off, but she didn't dare ask him to lower his hand even for a moment. By the blood splashed around the boat, it looked as if he should be dead by now. . . . From the other boat Brian asked shakily, "Can you do it, Clarie?"

"Hand me something to twist this with, will you?"

"Sure, sure . . . but, *what?*"

"Screwdriver." Owen bit off the word. Brian scrambled for it and handed it across to her.

"There," Clarie said.

"By gorry, girl, she's slacking up," Owen said. He breathed as if he had been afraid to breathe for some time. "I didn't know but what all they'd find of me would be a puddle."

"You can hold that yourself, can't you?" Clarie asked him.

He took hold of the screwdriver and then gave her a facsimile of his own smile. "Yep. That's the finest kind."

"You're supposed to loosen it every so often," she said, remembering what was said in the first-aid book.

"I know that much." Owen gave her a bigger grin.

"Is your engine broken down?" she asked him. "Will we have to take you in tow?"

"No, I shut her off to tend to my hand. I was mending a hole in a traphead. The boat fetched a lurch that near sent me off my feet, and drove the knife into my wrist just as I was reaching in to cut the twine." The trap was still there, across the top of a barrel.

Clarie drew air into her cramped chest. "One of us will go in with you and the other can take our boat. I don't know anything about this engine, so I guess Brian'd better go with you."

"*Me?*" Brian gasped.

"What's the matter, sonny? You scared I'll die on ye?"

73

"Come on, Brian," Clarie said, taking the gaff from him and hooking onto *Sea Dancer*'s rail. "Mind the deck, it's slippery."

Giving her an agonized look, Brian scrambled across, and she climbed back aboard *Sea Dancer*. "Owen, if you think you might faint put your head down to your knees," Clarie said.

"Why can't we take our boat in tow?" Brian beseeched her. She unhooked the gaff and laid it on the washboard.

"How much time would we make that way? We'd better go straight to Brigport. The district nurse can take over then. She'll know if he needs a doctor." Clarie gave him an encouraging nod and a small grin, to hide the reaction that was now making her feel as pale and shaky as Brian looked.

She started up *Sea Dancer,* and Brian started *White Lady.* "Owen'll let you run her wide open!" she called to him. *White Lady* sprang away from *Sea Dancer,* dipped her nose in a sea, rose up shaking herself and headed on a straight course past the Eastern End of Bennett's toward Brigport, a mile and a half away. Her wake foamed out magnificently behind and gave *Sea Dancer* a chance to live up to her name.

Clarie's legs were trembling and her hands were clammy. She thought wryly that she should be wild with delight at having the boat to herself, but instead she was worrying about events aboard *White Lady.* She tried to remember if Owen had looked gray; that could mean he'd lost a great amount of blood. If he should faint in spite of her instructions and keel over, and start bleeding

74

again—sweat ran down her back at the picture and at the thought of Brian's terror. She'd been in command, but had she done the right thing? Should they have anchored *Sea Dancer* and both have gone with Owen? It was too late now for that. *White Lady*'s top speed was so much faster than *Sea Dancer*'s that she could never hope to catch up.

White Lady was rolling in the deep wash off the Head and throwing spray over herself in great showers. Clarie strained to see if there were two figures upright in the cockpit; at least Brian was still at the wheel. Then a burst of rain obscured the windshield for a few moments and when it ran off *White Lady* was no longer in sight.

"They'll be all right," she said aloud. "Of course they'll be all right." This was one of the moments in life when you wished you could escape, simply fly miraculously away from all feelings of responsibility and act as if they had never been.

On the edge of her vision, to the left, something dark seemed to rise or surge. She swung her head quickly in panic, and saw Ross Bennett's boat abreast of her, and coming closer. She saw the gaff in his hand and knew he wanted to come alongside. She slowed *Sea Dancer* down to a mere forward drift.

"What's happened?" he shouted at her as the two boats drew together. "Where's Brian?"

She pointed. "Almost into Brigport Harbor by now, I hope! We found Owen drifting around out here with a bad gash in his wrist, and Brian went with him."

"I thought you'd lost him overboard. Usually he's the one steering. . . . You look pretty sick."

"I'm feeling pretty sick." She was glad to admit it, dignity or not.

Ross sat on the washboard of his boat and took out his pipe, as if they were passing the time of day in summer sunlight on dry land, and she sank down on the engine box.

"How bad was it?"

"I don't know if it was an artery or not. I fixed a tourniquet for him, but there was a lot of blood. I've been worrying about that." It was a relief to pass on the worry, even to Ross Bennett.

"A little blood can splash around and look like a gallon or so, and I guess Owen's got plenty to spare," he said. "If it was an artery you did the right thing, and if it wasn't I guess you didn't do him any harm."

She began to feel better. "I told Brian to go to Brigport. Mrs. Thomson can take care of it and see if he needs a doctor. I was following."

"I'll go over. Want to come aboard and we'll take your boat in tow?"

"In one way I'd like to," she said honestly. "But I don't very often get her away from Brian."

They smiled at each other, and he stood up and unhooked his gaff. "No need of you going to Brigport unless you want to. Will you be insulted if I tell you not to get reckless and see how close you can run by the Head?"

"Nope! Because I don't intend to do that. I'm going to be way, way out, man."

She didn't hear what he said but saw the flash of his teeth as he laughed. They started their engines and now

76

she could enjoy the sensation of command as the boat sprang to life. The wash and surge around the base of the great bare knob of pale rock known as the Head spread outward even farther than she'd expected, and the boat rose high and sank low and was sometimes roughly nudged or jolted, but she eased *Sea Dancer* through it in professional fashion, and even managed to glance around as if she were far more casual than she felt. She waved at *Moonlight* to show her nonchalance. Look, Ma, only one hand on the wheel! she thought with a grin.

Then she was around the Head and passing suddenly into lee waters. The engine throbbed sweetly as *Sea Dancer* glided by Eastern End Cove and Steve Bennett's home and anchorage. She kept remembering how glad she'd been to see Ross and dump everything onto him. And he had taken the load and made her feel better at once. He *is* nice, she thought repentantly. I don't know what there is about him that makes me act so, sometimes.

In the harbor the air was warm and springlike after the rawness outside in the wind. As she came up to the car, Mark called, "Hey! Where's your kid brother? Didn't bait a trap with him, did ye?"

She laughed and then quickly sobered. "He's gone to Brigport with Owen." She told him the rest of it.

"I'll call up the store over there and see what they can tell me, and then I'd better talk to his wife." Mark reached for the first crate.

"You don't have to tend to these now," Clarie objected. "Go on and call up."

"Nope. We'll get these lobsters out of the way first.

Don't know what good a call can do anyway. Ross is there on the spot." He slid the crate onto the scales, and adjusted the weight, scowling. "Good thing you kids happened along, I'd say."

That was rather nice to hear. She'd be sure to pass it on to Brian. While Mark figured on a pad she leaned on the scales and watched a few gulls paddling tamely close to the car. She felt a rare peace compounded of many things, the sunshine, Mark's praise, running the boat, the meeting with Ross. . . .

Mark pulled out the thick roll of bills always in his pocket for buying lobsters, and paid her. "Your news knocked mine clean out of my head," he said. "You folks had company come out on the boat today. Your mother wasn't down to the wharf, so I pointed him in the right direction."

Unexpected company. A man. . . . Her father had cousins who lived in the South—it could be one of them. What courage to visit us in February! Clarie thought. Happily she did the necessary home-coming chores at the Tanner wharf, then went back out to the mooring to make the boat secure. The harbor was in the lee today or she'd never have been able to do this alone, but she managed to guess the exact moment for cutting off the engine and hooking up the mooring buoy before the boat could slide past it. I wish Ross had seen that, she thought more with pride than with malice.

The memory of their meeting stayed with her as she rowed ashore. The children were out of school and playing outdoors, crows yammered over the woods, and gulls banked and glided over the harbor. Clarie walked contentedly to the house, carrying a basket of lobsters they'd saved out for supper. Hodge was sitting on the front steps in the sun, and he chirruped and came to meet her, then ran ahead of her along the walk to the back door. "Look, Hodgy, lobsters," she told him, tilting down the basket. Hodge commenced his loud bubbly purr. "There's a whole one for you," said Clarie, "so we can eat ours in peace, not in pieces."

They went in through the entry and she opened the kitchen door and let him in first. Her mother said, "Well, old Hodge-podge." A man laughed. Disbelief dried Clarie's throat. Trembling, she shifted a weakened grip on the basket and went in to meet Paul.

9

HE STOOD UP to meet her, thinly elegant in narrow-legged black pants and a wine-colored pinwale shirt. She'd always admired the way he wore his clothes, and she remembered that in this moment of struggle to make his presence here *real*. He was here in this kitchen, flesh and blood, clothes you could touch, one-sided smile and bright hazel eyes, hair flopping across his forehead in the way she loved. He wasn't an apparition conjured up by a longing heart. He was here, her hand was in his, and he held it tightly.

"Hello, Clarie," he said.

"Hello, Paul. What a surprise!" It sounded weak and artificial. "I brought in some lobsters, and I didn't even know we had company."

"I'd better put some water on," her mother said. "If *you're* surprised, imagine how I felt when someone knocked at the door and this strange young man stood there, just like in the city." Paul joined in her laughter.

"She thought I was selling vacuum cleaners or encyclopedias," he explained. "She was torn between compassion because I looked so pale after my trip, and horror that Creeping Suburbia had crept way out here."

"I see compassion won," said Clarie. She was beginning to function again, taking off her jacket, making futile gestures at her rumpled hair.

"Clarie, you look terrific!" He had a way of making his eyes seem to light up; she had never figured out how he did it. "I thought all this wind and weather turned people leathery, but you're blooming like a rose."

"My secret is that I keep a mare in the shed and wash my face every night with her milk," explained Clarie. "Well, if you'll excuse me I'll go change out of my work clothes."

"And I'll make a pot of coffee," said her mother. Her cheeks were attractively flushed, and she seemed almost lighthearted. Well, Paul was a good conversationalist, and he knew how to draw people out. How well Clarie knew that he could draw people out. . . .

Peeling off in her room, she realized that he had come and surprised her just as she had dreamed of his coming. But she did not feel the painful ecstasy she had experienced in the daydreams. In fact the numbing astonishment at sight of him had been so unpleasant that now she was almost reluctant to go downstairs.

Oh, don't be so foolish! she flared at herself. She put on slim blue slacks and a matching shirt, brushed her black hair hard, and went downstairs again. Paul was setting out the cups and telling Mrs. Tanner about the shop.

"I know Clarie really loved it," Mrs. Tanner said regretfully. "Oh, here she is. What's holding up your brother?"

Clarie told her, glad to have something to talk about. A warm apple pie was placed on the table, chairs drawn up. Finally Clarie managed to ask Paul in a more or less

81

natural manner what had brought him out on the boat.

"Why, I came to see you," he said with a smile. "Isn't that excuse enough?"

"An excuse isn't a reason, so I've been taught."

"Well, the reason is that we miss you. Not only the family, but the customers, and everybody in the block. So I thought, Now it's February, and by gum she ought to be tired enough of battling the elements to come back and gladden all our hearts."

"Listen to that, Clarie!" Margaret was laughing.

Clarie pretended to be watching the harbor for the return of *Moonlight* and *White Lady*. What about Dottie Dimples? she questioned passionately in silence. How do you have the gall to walk in here shedding charm like mad after what you did to me?

"Want to take a walk, Paul?" she said. "I hate to settle down in the house when I've been in the boat all day, unless it's really cold and nasty. It's nice out now."

"I'd like it," said Paul.

She wanted to get him away from the harbor as quickly as possible, before the men began coming in. To show him off as her accepted boy friend was one thing, but now she couldn't bear the well-meaning smiles and jokes that his presence would provoke.

"Let's go across the island," she suggested. "I can show you the school, and—"

"Hey!" It was Brian, coming out between the fish-houses. He gave Paul a quizzical and friendly grin. "Who's this?"

Clarie introduced them and asked about Owen.

82

"Gone in to Limerock," he said. "Ross went too. Say, your tourniquet really worked, Clarie," he told her with admiration. "But Mrs. Thomson said he needed a doctor, all right, so we had the plane come out for him. And whatdya know, Ross let me bring his boat home. There she is, on her own mooring, snug and safe. Hey, what's to eat?"

"Fresh apple pie," said Paul. "Your mother was taught to cook by angels in heaven."

"Get *him!*" said Brian. He went whistling up the walk to the back door, and Clarie and Paul went toward the harbor beach. When they started across the marsh, he put his arm around her waist.

She stiffened. "The teacher's still there, can't you see her?"

"What's the difference?" He glanced toward the schoolhouse windows. "We used to walk up Main Street hand in hand, as I remember, and you didn't worry then."

"That was different." She felt prickly and overwarm, irritable all over, and it wasn't supposed to be that way. She was walking on the island with Paul, *with Paul,* and he wanted to put his arm around her. "Everything was different over there," she protested.

"I know, at home you're self-conscious, you feel everyone's watching you," Paul said. "It's inhibiting. But don't you get a big bang out of making them stare and wonder?"

"I've had enough of it since my father died," she said dryly. "Nobody thought Brian and I were capable of doing what we've done, and nobody was a bit backward in saying so. But we've proved ourselves now."

"Then if you've proved yourself now, you should be ready for the next step," said Paul. They went across the schoolyard and down to the beach before she stopped and faced him.

"What next step?"

"Come back, Clarie," he whispered. He put his hands on her waist. "Come back. Everybody misses you, but I do most of all."

The sun was too hot through her jacket, and Paul's fingers pressed too hard against her ribs. "What's the matter with Dottie Dimples?" she asked, louder than she'd intended.

"Who?"

"Your girl friend. When I was a kid my mother gave me some paper dolls she used to play with, and there was this one named Dottie Dimples. Big smile, curls, and dimples an inch deep."

He began to laugh. "A paper doll! That's perfect! I must have been some kind of a nut, and don't think I haven't had to eat crow by the flock. My father and mother hardly spoke to me for weeks, and by that time I'd found out all there was to know about—Dottie Dimples." His face blazed up. He pulled her into his arms and kissed her. "I've missed you for so long," he murmured. "I couldn't stand it any more."

She felt the old fire, and then, swiftly, as if something else besides herself were in control, it was quenched. She moved her face away from his and got out of his arms after a slight struggle. "I think we'd better walk," she said.

"Why should we, after all this time? Let's find ourselves a nice warm rock out of the public eye."

"A warm rock in February?"

"Don't be so practical. This could be a gorgeous tropical island with only you and me on it."

"And any minute now a tribe of natives can burst down on us from either that house"—she pointed to the Homestead—"or from that." She pointed in the opposite direction, to the roofs of Hillside Farm.

"Then let's go up in those woods, where you won't be so stiff and self-conscious." He kissed her under the ear and she pulled her head away, incredulous at her own act. How could she behave this way to Paul, who had pleaded with her just exactly as she had wanted him to plead?

"Well, we have to walk to the woods, we can't fly," she said, "so let's start walking." She put her arm through his and set him in motion along the beach.

He said ardently. "You're coming back, aren't you? You could go back with me on the mailboat. I know your mother wouldn't mind, I don't think she's too keen on this lobstering kick of yours."

Be calm, she admonished herself. Be logical. Be adult. "Look, Paul, I couldn't decide anything on the spur of the moment like this. I couldn't walk out of here in two days. I couldn't walk out on Brian, period. We've got three hundred traps out there, and a good business going."

"But it's only temporary, isn't it?" he argued. "You can't keep it up forever. Your brother ought to be in school, and your mother could get a good job." He stopped their walk and turned her around to face him. "Look, you never planned on making a career of this. You only got into it because of what I did, didn't you? Because you wanted to get out of Limerock?"

"I did not!" she blazed at him. "I wanted to look out for my mother! Brian and I both did!"

"You mean," he asked skeptically, "that if I hadn't flipped over the paper dolly you wouldn't still be right over there in the shop happy as a clam at high water?"

"Yes, that's what I mean! I knew what my duty was!"

"Who or what are you trying to drown out, honey?"

"You, maybe!" This was fire of a different sort. "You tell me it was nice knowing me, so long, kid, and then six months later you come sailing across the bay like Columbus and say, Oh, I made a mistake, come back, I can't stand it! Well, I had to make my life over last September, without my father in it and without *you* in it, and I can't make it into something else in three days or even three weeks just because you say so!"

"Calm down, calm down." Gently he shook her. But he wasn't smiling. "Just tell me the truth in a few simple words. Are you glad I showed up or aren't you?"

"I don't know what I think," she retorted.

"Well, then, there's no point in finding us a snug nook in the woods, is there?"

"None at all." She stared at a clan of old-squaws diving in splashes of silver.

86

"Too bad I couldn't get back tonight," said Paul.

"Yes, isn't it?" She turned abruptly and started up over the beach, not looking to see if he followed. The time between now and next boatday stretched out longer than all the days since she had last seen Paul, and in a way it would be much worse. To have him here with this dreadful cold and ache between them. . . . She whirled suddenly, and almost bumped into him.

"Oh, Paul, don't let's be mad!" she exclaimed. "I've been a perfectly awful hostess so far, I admit it."

His remote expression disappeared. "Well, what you said about my coming out here and thinking I could make everything over in one day was the truth. I deserved it."

"Then can we just have a good time while you're here and not get worked up about anything?"

"I can't promise about that—" He reached for her and she put her hands on his chest.

"You've got to promise. I've too many responsibilities now to make snap decisions. Last year there was just me. Now there's my mother and Brian."

"Sure, honey, I know." He squeezed her hands, and then pulled her arm through his. "All right, I promise."

10

BEFORE THE HOUSE quieted down for the night, Paul, Clarie, and Brian bundled up and walked out onto the far end of Mark Bennett's wharf. The cloudiness had cleared completely before a north-west wind that smelled of March rather than January. Brian flashed a strong light on the moorings, and one boat after another shone against the dark. "There's our girl."

"I wish I'd seen Clarie bringing her home."

"Everybody but Mark missed that stirring sight," said Clarie. "You should've seen me put her on the mooring, Brian."

"Ahuh," he grunted. "One little bounce and you'd have gone right headfirst over the bow. But no, you couldn't wait till I came home. Had to do it all alone to show you could."

"Oh, fie upon you, as they say in old books. I was running around the washboards when you were still in diapers."

Paul cleared his throat ostentatiously. "Would anybody like to hear about me and skis?" he asked. In the dark and during their laughter his fingers squeezed Clarie's arm just above the elbow, and she didn't move away.

"Listen to the water sloshing under the wharf," she said dreamily. "And down on the west side the surf will be gleaming in the starlight there, with nobody to watch it."

"Let's go, he cried recklessly through chattering teeth," said Paul.

"Serve you right if I took you up on it," said Clarie. "But all of a sudden my day's catching up with me. If I get up the stairs without falling asleep I'll do well."

They didn't go to haul the next day. The lobster catches were growing smaller, as happened several times during the year, and once a string of gear was hauled through it was common sense to let the well-baited traps set over for several days. Instead they took *Sea Dancer* out to entertain Paul with a trip around the island.

Clarie watched him as he stood by the wheel and followed Brian's pointing finger and explanations. Do I love him? she asked herself, and waited for the flooding *Yes, yes, yes!* But it didn't come, only a painful confusion compounded of sweet memories and bitter ones. I'm afraid to admit it, she thought; I went into it headlong in the first place, like falling downstairs, and took an awful crack on my head at the bottom of it. But he's learned, he swears he has. I'm the one, he says. *The one*.

"Let's go around by Brigport harbor on the way back," she suggested. "We can show Paul the picturesque inhabitants and go browsing in the native shops."

"Do they have beautiful girls swim out to meet the boats and throw wreaths of flowers around our necks?"

"Wreaths of baitbags," suggested Brian. "Full of herring."

They kept their foolishness going as they came into Brigport harbor. "Say, I've never been this close to an outrigger canoe," Paul marveled when they passed by a forty-foot seiner.

"Hey, there's the Kon-Tiki!" Brian pointed at a dory.

"Viking long ship," said Paul when they slid under the bow of a visiting lobster smack. "Either they've missed their century, or we have."

The long wharf at Brigport was deserted in the late-morning quiet. It wasn't a boatday, and the men who weren't out hauling were working in their fishhouses along the edges of the narrow harbor. A couple of them were out aboard the lobster smack, *Gypsy Queen,* talking with the crew.

"This way to the native quarter," Clarie said, pointing to the store on the rise of land. "Delicious exotic food and drink."

Arm in arm, Paul in the middle, exhilarated by sun and laughter, they went up the wharf. Just as they approached the store Paul stopped dramatically.

"I'll be goldurned," he breathed. "There's one of the fellers that must have come on the Viking ship."

It was Jamie coming around the corner, with his watch cap on the back of his yellow head.

"Hi, Leif Erickson!" Brian sang out.

"Hi," Jamie responded with a notable lack of enthusiasm.

For some reason Clarie was embarrassed. She pulled her arm out of Paul's and said hurriedly, "Jamie, I want you to meet Paul Ryder. It was his mother and father I

90

worked for over in Limerock. Paul, this is Jamie Sorensen."

They shook hands, Jamie polite but noncommittal,
Paul very friendly. "They sent me out to get Clarie
back," he said.

"You having any success?"

"I can't tell yet," said Paul. "She's a mysterious crit-
ter."

"You over here alone, Leif?" Brian asked.

"Brought my mother over to see somebody. Well, I
guess I'll go out aboard the *Queen* and see if it's true
what I just heard."

"What was that?" Clarie asked brightly.

"They're up here from the west'ard and offering a dollar a pound for lobsters. Tom Robey's in the store chewing his fingers clear back to the wrists."

Brian whistled. "A dollar!"

"Don't go all to pieces," Clarie advised him. "They
won't be here for long. I've heard about these deals before and so have you."

"Excuse, please," said Paul, "but I don't speak the
language. Either use English, or direct me to the Ameri-
can consul."

"Well, this buyer has come from somewhere else, and
anchored here to buy what lobsters he can," Clarie exclaimed, "and he'll probably get quite a few of those
brought in today, because he's offering something above
the going price. Tom Robey's the buyer here, and he's
having a fit."

"Chomping his fingers down knuckle by knuckle," said

91

Paul. "I see. But why do they let this other type muscle in here?"

"Nobody can stop him from anchoring, or the men from selling to him. Oh, some won't, they'll be loyal to Tom because he's here all the time, you see, and he sees that they get bait, and so forth. This smack may never come back here again."

"But there'll be some who'll go after that extra ten or fifteen cents," Jamie said.

"I'd be one of 'em if I was over here," said Brian fervently. "That's an extra ten or fifteen dollars on every hundred pounds, boy."

"What would you do with it?" Jamie asked. "Spend it on cigareets and whuskey and wild, wild wimmen?" They all laughed, then Jamie nodded at Paul and said, "Nice to meet you. So long." He went on down the wharf.

"Silent type, but he did melt down a bit finally," said Paul.

"Too bad we couldn't have a dance while you're here, and then you'd know just how silent they really are," said Clarie.

"Summer is when we have the best dances," said Brian, "either here or over home, and people come from as far away as Vinalhaven, or even Isle au Haut sometimes. That's the time, boy. Summer."

Yes, summer, Clarie thought. Last summer I was going to take Paul to a clubhouse dance. We'd have gone outdoors when we didn't want to dance. In the early summer you smell the wild roses strong at night, and see the fireflies; in late summer there's the scent of apples under the wild trees behind the clubhouse, and if you get a little distance away from the music you hear the crickets.   There would have been a full moon on dance night when Paul was here.

"Coming in, doll?"   Paul touched her ear, and smiled into her bemused eyes.   "How are things, sweetie?" he whispered.   She smiled at him, she hoped enigmatically, and went ahead of him into the store.

At home in the afternoon Brian wanted to show Paul some of the shoreline, and though Clarie knew Paul would rather go alone with her, she was so agreeable to Brian's suggestions that both boys gave her rather curious glances.

They went past the schoolhouse and Owen Bennett's house into the woods, then along a path high above the surf to the Eastern End, where Steve Bennett's property lay in the gentle hollow between southerly and northerly shores.   They visited Steve in his fishhouse so Paul could see a trap being built.   Steve was the youngest of the Bennett brothers, and the quietest, and he made Clarie think of Ross.   She wondered why she hadn't noticed it before.

From there they climbed among ledge and spruce to the top of the Head and sat there surveying the great blue plain of sea which stretched away from them to a clear-cut horizon line except where it was broken by the mainland hills in the north, and Isle au Haut rising from the water like a mystic mountain.

Then they came back to the harbor, bought soda pop and potato chips, and went out on Mark's wharf to watch the home-coming boats and the sale of lobsters. To make it more interesting, the Fisheries launch arrived, bringing two wardens to make a routine check of the hauls.

Ross Bennett had come out with them. Clarie, sitting between Paul and Brian on the edge of the wharf, felt a peculiar self-consciousness. Her mind went blank; it was as if a transparent but soundproof wall had suddenly set her off from the boys on either side of her so that she was isolated, and in a weird way she was also isolated from herself. On the car below them Ross was telling Mark that the doctor wanted to keep an eye on Owen but he would probably be home by the end of the week.

Then Mark turned back to business, and Ross came to the ladder. "Hi, Ross!" Brian greeted him, very friendly since he'd run *Moonlight* yesterday.

Ross gave him a sober nod. "Hello, Brian . . . Clarie." His eyes moved toward Paul, dark and unreadable. He did not smile, and Clarie could have let him go on up the wharf without another look in her direction. Afterward she wondered why she didn't. Instead she put her hands lightly on the boys' shoulders and stood up, saying, "Wait a minute, Ross, I'd like you to meet Paul Ryder."

Paul got up too, smiling, his hand out. "Paul Ryder, Ross Bennett," Clarie said, and they shook hands. Take a good look, Ross, she thought. This is the one. And you can think what you want to. . . . It was a foolish, meaningless sort of defiance. She couldn't understand it and was ashamed of it, and so she was angry with Ross who, however, appeared too preoccupied to notice anything.

94

"This is a great place," said Paul. "I can see now why Clarie's half gull."

"Is she?" said Ross dryly.

"Sheds feathers all the time," Brian contributed. Ross nodded at Paul. "Glad to meet you."

They watched him go up the wharf. "Grim chap," Paul observed.

"Not really," said Clarie, wishing she hadn't stopped Ross; just by standing there being remote he'd made her feel foolish, and she didn't know whether to blame him or herself. When he'd come along yesterday after Owen's accident it hadn't been anything like this. "He's just quiet," she heard herself saying. "He's probably tired."

"We islanders never sleep good off on the mainland," Brian said.

"You mean he wasn't actually unfriendly toward this pesky off-islander?" asked Paul with a grin. "I'd say he was pretty suspicious, and I don't blame him. I'd be the same way about city slickers."

"You make him sound like a—a country bumpkin," Clarie knew she was too indignant, but she couldn't seem to help it. "He has something on his mind, probably, and you hardly registered."

"Ross *is* kind of deep," Brian said importantly. "Oh, he bugs me sometimes, chasing us around as if we needed a nursemaid, but I believe in giving the devil his due."

"Say, that's darned white of you," said Paul. Brian chuckled, and something which had risen under a tranquil surface to threaten that tranquillity subsided again.

95

11

In the evening Paul wanted to learn the knot used for trapheads and baitbags, and worked at it until he could do it with ease and speed. They talked, laughed some more, ate and sang. It was fun, but now Clarie wanted him to go without cornering her for any more definite answers, and when she woke in the morning she was glad it was a fine day so that the mailboat would come.

"After a couple of days out here I'm going to have claustrophobia in the shop," Paul said at breakfast. "I know now why islanders stay islanders, no matter where they go."

"Well, we've certainly enjoyed you, Paul," Mrs. Tanner said. "You must come again."

"Thank you, I won't let you forget that." He gave Clarie a smile of purest innocence. "Can't we take another walk?"

"As long as you're back for an eleven o'clock lunch," her mother said. "The boat leaves at twelve."

"And it's better to have a full stomach if you're seasick," said Brian helpfully. "When you have to heave over the side, it's easier if you have something to heave."

"Brian, why don't you get to work?" suggested his mother.

"I was going with them."

96

"Your schoolwork, Brian. You didn't do a thing yes-terday."

Clarie had wanted to invite him, but she couldn't say anything now, not after her lectures and harangues about his lessons. He collapsed groaning on the couch as they left. In front of the house they discussed destinations.

"We haven't time to do the Western End," Clarie said, glad of that. She pounced giddily on a way to kill time. "Come on, let's go look at Charles Bennett's boat."

They walked toward the long shed where smoke was already rising from the stovepipe through the roof. "Charles Bennett is the oldest brother," she explained. "Philip's the next, but he doesn't live here. Then Owen —he's the one who cut his wrist. Jamie's mother comes in there, then Mark Bennett, and Steve, at the Eastern End. Sometimes I wish I'd been alive when they were all kids here. It must have been terrific."

"Where does this Ross Bennett come in?" It was an innocent question, but was it too innocent? She looked at him sidewise, and his expression told her nothing.

"He's a cousin. Ross's father left here and went down east to settle, but Ross came back a few years ago. He boards over at Hillside with Owen's family."

"Bachelor, huh? Is he scared of women?"

"How should I know?" She laughed to hide an unrea-sonable annoyance. "Why?"

"Idle curiosity, my girl, that's all. Not many like him are still loose at his age, so I wondered."

"What do you mean, like him?"

"Well, he's a good-looking guy, and probably makes

plenty of money out here, to judge by his boat and what you've told me about the lobstering here. But he's still a bachelor and you can't hardly find that kind no more."

He seemed amused by himself, so she smiled too. "Oh, he may be engaged to somebody on the mainland, for all we know. You know what Brian says, 'Ross is kind of deep.' He'll go ashore some day and come back with a wife on his arm and a boatload of furniture, and a deed to one of the empty houses. Anyway, what difference does it make? I thought that only girls were nosy about other people's marriage prospects."

He gave her a particularly charming smile. "Maybe I've got a right to be nosy. Ever think of that?"

"Why have you got a right?" she demanded.

"I saw the way he looked at you the other day, and I saw the way he looked at me. He had a hard eye, girl. A hard eye."

"I never heard of anything so silly!" she protested. "I never knew you were like this, Paul." She decided to be sadly shocked at this revelation of his character.

"And why was he preoccupied, my sweet? Because he saw *you* with *me*. Are you blushing?"

"Only with rage!" She felt like slapping him. "I never heard a man sound so—so *petty,* and *foolish,* and *ridiculous,* and—"

"Go on, sputter," he said calmly. He opened the door of the boat shop and thrust her inside, and she was forced into a fiery silence.

Charles was alone this morning and she introduced Paul, whose intelligent questions made Charles talk more than he usually did.   Clarie sat on a nail keg and played a checker game against herself, won it, and started another game.   As long as the men could keep up this ardent conversation about boats, she was safe.   *Safe.*   What a sadly ironic word to use where Paul was concerned.

Charles had to transfer operations to the inside of the hull after a while, so the discussion ended.   By then a small dragger and a Coast Guard cutter had arrived in company at Mark's wharf, so they walked around there to see what the story was.   The dragger had sprung a leak and the pumps weren't working properly, so she had called for help, and the cutter was escorting her home. They'd stopped in at Bennett's to see if they could put the pumps in temporary repair before the twenty-five mile trip to the mainland.

"I can see where a little excitement goes a long way around here," said Paul.   "Let's go for a walk where you wouldn't go in the dark the other night, and create some excitement of our own."

She looked hopefully at her watch, and was rewarded. "I'd love to, but it's too near eleven."   As if to back her up, the mailboat whistle sounded behind Eastern Harbor Point.   "I guess we'd better wait and pick up the mail, and by then it'll be time to eat."

"When do I get a chance to talk to you?"   He was no longer so pleased with everything and himself.

"Let's sit on a crate way out at the end," she suggested, hoping that one of the women coming to meet the boat would interrupt them.   But it was a faint hope, because everyone would be much too tactful.   Probably they

99

hope he's sweeping me off my feet so I'll be ready to give up this unwomanly life, she thought nastily. Young Lochinvar out of the West. At this point I'd settle for the merman and his ceiling of amber.

"What are you thinking?" Paul said in her ear. "I can't tell if you're savage or sad."

"A little of both, maybe." The mailboat crossed the harbor, looking brave and salty and sea-going.

"Do you love me?"

"I don't know." She gazed at the boat until the silence had lasted too long, and then she looked sidewise at him. He was actually pale; with anger, or anguish? "Paul, that's the truth," she said earnestly. "I don't know. Maybe if our breakup hadn't come when it did, when my father died, it wouldn't have thrown me so hard. But it did, and for a long time all I knew was that I didn't ever want to take a chance on that happening to me again, with anyone."

"But Clarie," he said huskily, "it *couldn't* happen to us again. I wouldn't let it! This time I want to marry you."

The word shot through her. She couldn't even repeat it, but stared silently at him, while she saw, like the shifting designs in a kaleidoscope, a rapid succession of scenes showing Life with Paul. Her stomach felt as if it were being delicately walked upon. The whole thing was absolutely incredible. Clarie married to Paul would be someone whom she did not know and could not imagine. Certainly she wouldn't be this girl sitting on a lobster crate on Bennett's Island. This girl would become a memory, and then a fading dream until she might never have existed at all.

"Well, Clarie?" Paul said. The wash of the mailboat was louder than her throttled engine as she approached the wharf.

Clarie had to clear her throat. "I never thought of marriage."

"Are you afraid of it?"

"Not exactly. *Respectful* is the word, but maybe that's not strong enough." Shaken by sincerity she exclaimed softly, "Paul, it's a—a giant step, it's like shooting for the moon!" But in the face of his tender amusement she gave up. He would have refuted everything she tried to say. "Well, anyway," she said, "I'm not telling you anything yet. Marriage concerns the rest of your life, and if you don't think that's like shooting for the moon you're a dreamer. I'm not saying 'yes' as if you'd just asked me to go out for hamburgers." She stood up. "There goes the mail up to the store. We'd better go now."

He was gone, taking it for granted that all Clarie wanted was time. Walking back from the wharf she wondered what she did want. She was only sure of what she didn't want: to be rushed, to be forced to give up what she had started and entrust herself to Paul.

There the pain lay, and it stirred in her as she went along with her head down and her hands in her pockets. Paul could still move her with a turn of the head, a certain expression around his mouth, something in his voice, the way his eyes lit up. But always there was this reluctance dragging at her like heavy water-soaked clothing. In these last few days she had longed to be free of it. *I run, I run, I am gathered to thy heart,* went a line of a poem in Brian's anthology. What must it be like to run thus, with no regrets and no fear?

A pebble landed on the path before her. She stared at it resentfully, as if it had waked her from a dream. Rubber boots came into her lowered circle of vision, and she raised her eyes and saw Jamie. She was close by the Sorensen fishhouse.

"I didn't know but what I'd have to fire a bigger one at you to get your attention," he said. "Want to go for a walk, now that you've got rid of Fancy Pants?"

She blinked at him. The other walk had been fun, but today it would cheat both of them. "Not today," she said. "I've let things go, I've got ironing and mending to do or else I'll be running out of clothes."

"Poor time of year for that," he said. "Well, I'll try again."

Oh, darn it! she thought angrily, why can't I like him the way he wants me to? Then, illogically, she was mad at Jamie for not being mad with her. It would be a load off her conscience if he'd get fed up and ignore her from now on.

"See you, Jamie," she said with a quick smile, and went on.

Brian was just coming out and she caught his arm as he went past her. "How about going out and hauling a few? The afternoons are a lot longer now."

"I'm going to Brigport with Hugo. He's got his father's boat." He started on, but she held onto his sleeve.

"We've wasted enough time and it may blow hard tomorrow. You can't tell, this time of year."

"So what?" He was beginning to get impatient. He'd studied all morning and was full of virtue and vigor. "Let 'em set over. They're slacking off anyway, you know that. Nobody else is out."

"Joey's out. So are Mr. Fennell and Ralph Percy."

He pulled his arm free, still good-natured in spite of his eagerness to be gone. "Look, sister mine, there are times when the only lobster traps I can stand to look at are the ones piled up on dry land."

"It'll be nice out there," she insisted. Paul wouldn't be out there either, attacking her with doubts and demands. She could become herself again, *Clarie,* hard, confident, sure of what she was doing. Her face must have shown something, for Brian said suddenly, "Hey! You really like him, don't you? You're missing him already."

"No, I'm not." She was careful not to snap.

He patted her cheek and went off toward the harbor beach. She stood watching him out of sight and wondered what to do. Nothing moved for a few moments in the sun-washed noon. For an instant even the gulls were not circling overhead. The silence and emptiness were repeated in Clarie's mind. Up until a few days ago she had thought she knew exactly what and who she was, and what she wanted. Now she knew nothing, nothing at all.

Suddenly something else was in the isolated moment with her. The black Labrador came trotting along by the fishhouses, his coat shining in the sun. When he saw her he stopped and looked at her with thoughtful amber eyes, then wagged his tail slightly. She put out her hand and he came to her. Under her fingers his hide was satiny-warm.

"You're nice," she said to him. "You know that? Right now you're about the nicest person I know, except maybe for Hodge."

12

THEY HAD three days of gale-force north-west winds, and then a day of gray calm that promised snow. Clarie was anxious to get started out again, but Brian dragged back. "There's no hurry," he said maddeningly, filling his plate for the second time. "The days are a lot longer now, remember?"

"Not if there's a storm coming. We ought to haul all the way through in case we don't get out for another week. Come on, get going," she urged. Their mother, at her desk in the living room, was saying nothing, but Clarie was careful to keep the edge out of her voice. "What's the matter with you anyway?" she asked him. "You sure love to count the money when Mark pays it out."

"There are times, my good woman, when money isn't all that matters. That's when I think I've seen enough lobstering to do me for the rest of my life."

She grabbed her jacket off its hook and went out, snatching her oilclothes from the entry as she passed through. She hurried across the road to the fishhouse, where she pulled on her outdoor clothes and then warmed herself by hauling out the baskets of bait. Hodge, who had been vainly mouse-hunting under the fishhouse, joined her. "Look," she said, "everybody else is out ahead of us again. Oh, last fall he couldn't get enough of it. 'Hi diddle dee, a lobsterman I'll be!' " she sang. "Now you need dynamite to roust him out. And his mother thinks he's *tired*." Hodge blinked at her over his shoulder as he sank his claws into the chopping block. "Tired," Clarie muttered. "He never had it so good. If I was a boy fifteen with nothing more to worry about than *he* has—"

"You know what they say about people who talk to themselves," said Brian, coming out on the wharf.

"Well, it's the only way I ever can hear any common sense."

Brian yawned and leaned languidly against the hoisting mast. She straightened up to say something sarcastic, but he was looking away from her, his mouth drooping, his eyes oddly bleak. He could be missing Father, she thought guiltily. So she didn't say anything, but untied the skiff.

The water was a flat dull gray except when the sun burned through the high overcast to make a pale silver-gilt sheen. A quiet cold gnawed at fingers and toes. Because there had been neither capricious winds nor seas to hold them back, they hauled through their gear a little faster than usual, and were back in the harbor by mid-afternoon. The day had done for Clarie what she had hoped for; it had set Paul and the mainland a world away, and now she looked forward to getting into the house, warming up, reading; maybe she'd walk up to the Percies' later on and see Marjorie.

When they came up to the lobster car, *White Lady* was tied alongside. Mark and Owen Bennett came down from the store, looking alike with their big shoulders and dark coloring until they were close enough to separate, and then they were very different.

Owen held up his bandaged hand. "I dunno whether the community's planning to offer you a vote of thanks for your good deed or just the opposite," he said. "But personally I'm much obliged to you two."

"You are very welcome, sir," said Clarie.

"I left a little something at the house for you this morning. It's not much, when you figger how valuable I am, but it's a slight token of my esteem, as the feller says."

"Well, thanks," said Brian. "But we don't need any present for doing what we're supposed to. That doesn't mean I'm giving it back to you."

"You better not, because it won't fit me anyway."

"Well, if all the bowing and scraping is over with," said Mark, "I'd like to buy some lobsters." As he and Brian took hold of opposite ends of a crate, the boy said, "What's the price today?"

"Eighty-five. Heave 'er over."

"The *Gypsy Queen*'s offering a dollar."

"They still over at Brigport?" Mark didn't seem impressed. He began adjusting weights.

"They were yesterday, so Lew said." Lew was the engineer on the mailboat. "They told him they were laying over another day or so."

"Can't have filled his order yet," said Owen from the head of the ladder. "I guess everybody and his brother aren't rushing to sell to him."

"But fifteen cents more! That's fifteen dollars more a

hundred pounds!" Brian's voice took on a nervous tautness. "If they can pay a dollar, why can't everybody else?"

"Meaning me?" said Mark good-naturedly. "Well, sonny, the Birch Point lobster company isn't paying me any dollar a pound, so that's why I'm not paying it."

"But that's the price somewhere," Brian argued. "Or why would the *Gypsy Queen* be paying it?"

"Because he's trying to fill a rush order for some dealer down the coast," Owen said. "Lobsters are slacking off right now, and the dealer's probably got orders from plenty of big hotels and restaurants in New York and Connecticut, but he's got no lobsters to ship. So he'll pay anything."

"Come on, boy," said Mark. "Let's get that other crate over here." Brian didn't move. "Oh, for heaven's sake," Clarie muttered. "I'll help you, Mark."

"It's too heavy for you." He leaned an elbow on the scales. "Look here, son, if you want to sell to the *Gypsy Queen,* you go on right over there and sell. He'll be glad to see you, I imagine. For some reason he's not filling his quota very fast."

"Of course he doesn't want to sell to them!" said Clarie.

"I do want to sell to them!" Brian was red. "We can use the extra money as well as anybody! We *should* get a dollar a pound right here in our own harbor. If one man's willing to pay it the rest should. And if we can't get it at home, we'll go where we can get it."

Clarie was furious. The fact that the two men showed neither anger nor amusement only made it worse. "You sound like an idiot! Those people are fly-by-nights, you'll get nothing from them—"

"Except about thirty dollars more for our day's work. And I'm not so crazy about lobstering that I'm not going to get all I can out of it." He reached for the crate already on the car. "Grab hold, Clarie," he ordered crisply.

"I will not." She folded her arms. Otherwise she might have grabbed Brian and shaken him until his teeth rattled.

Mark took the other grip. "All right, heave away, boy." They swung the crate back onto the stern, Brian not looking at Mark.

"Are you going now?" Clarie asked him, tight-lipped.

"Right now."

"I'm not going with you."

Stiff with dignity, he untied the boat and stepped aboard. Burning hot, Clarie managed to watch steadily as he backed away at a higher speed than usual, the roar of the engine and explosive swirl of white water at her stern like a final burst of defiance. He was ostentatiously casual, giving the wheel a spin with one touch of his hand, swinging the bow around fast, heading out swiftly enough to set the big car lifting and falling in the after-wash.

"That's a hight in the hoot, if I ever saw one," Owen chuckled.

"He's a *brat*," said Clarie between her teeth. She started for the ladder, wanting only to get away from the men.

"You don't want to run off mad," Owen teased her.

"I could strangle him," she burst out. "What an exhibition! I was never so embarrassed in my life!"

"Well, don't be," said Mark. "He's only a young one, and he's ambitious. He's not the only one, either. I could name you two fishermen from this harbor who went over there yesterday. Looked everywhere but at me while they were gassing up this morning, too." He sounded amused.

"But you've always been so good to Brian—"

"Look, Mark won't go hungry from losing your lobsters for a day," said Owen. "Brian's all right. Got a lot on his mind. Let him run before the wind for a day or two, do him good." He spoke past her to his brother. "You should have seen him the other day. Scared feather-white for fear I'd up and die on him before we hit Brigport. That jaw was set some hard, I can tell you. It's a wonder his teeth weren't ground right down to the gums."

The tension began to go out of Clarie, and she smiled in spite of herself. "I was scared, too. I never saw so much blood in my life. I kept thinking of this line in a play we read at school. 'Who would have thought the old man had so much blood in him?' "

Owen threw back his head and laughed. Feeling a little better, Clarie left. She was not so wrought up now, but she was still displeased with Brian, no matter what they said. . . . Things on his mind, Owen said. What did he mean by that? She wished she'd asked him, but what could he know about Brian, after all?

When she went into the house her mother said, "Where's Brian? Didn't I see the boat going out of the harbor again?"

"He's gone to Brigport." The packages from Owen were on the table, the names scrawled blackly across the wrappings. She picked hers up.

"I suppose Brian's in an odd position, as a fifteen-year-old boy helping to earn the family living," said Mrs. Tanner, "but he *is* only fifteen, and I don't like the idea of his taking the boat and going whenever he feels like it, without getting permission first. Did you speak to him about it, Clarie?"

"I did," said Clarie, "but I was the last person he wanted to listen to. Some fly-by-night buyer from down the coast is over at Brigport offering a dollar a pound, and Brian is off in full cry, like a beagle after a rabbit." She observed her mother's dismay and said, "Mark was nicer about it than I was. Don't worry."

"Well, I *am* worried," Mrs. Tanner put down the bright wool she was knitting. "Brian does well for a while, and then he goes off half-cocked. I think I'm right about him, Clarie. He gets tired and then he's unreasonable." Here it came again. Clarie armed herself. Quickly she opened her package, rattling the paper loudly. It was a light-weight wind-proof parka of lustrous silky fabric. "Look at this!"

"It's lovely," agreed her mother. "How'd he ever manage to match your eyes so exactly?"

"I don't know, but he did such a good job it's almost a pity he's married, isn't it?" Clarie giggled at her

111

mother's expression. "He could be my first older man."

"I should think Paul could fill that post. He's twenty-two, he told me. . . . Did he ever show any signs of liking you, particularly, when you worked for his folks?"

"Oh, Paul likes all the girls." She was trying on the parka. "It's like that thing on the piano. 'I love coffee, I love tea, Paul likes the girls and the girls like he.' "

"They'll take you back whenever you want to go," said her mother.

"So he told me. But I don't want to go back. I'm here now." As her mother lifted a disturbed face, Clarie added hastily, "Until the end of this summer, anyway."

13

MARGARET TANNER took her knitting up to the Sorensens' and Clarie had a mug-up and then went upstairs to read. After a time when she looked up from her book she saw *Sea Dancer* at the mooring, and Brian up on the bow hooking up the buoy. She watched him objectively, no longer really cross with him but only hoping that he'd come in cheerful enough to quiet their mother's doubts.

He made the bow secure, then went aft where the crates were. He took hold of the end of one with both hands and slid the crate overboard.

"That crate's still full of lobsters!" Clarie said aloud, and Hodge stopped purring. The second crate was also heavy. He had them tied together so that they lay along the boat's side. When he rowed away from the big boat he was towing the crates behind him.

He hadn't sold, then. Maybe he'd thought better of it. But in that case why hadn't he gone directly back to the wharf and sold to Mark? He shipped his oars as he came to a buoy marking an empty mooring, and here he fastened the crates and then rowed on toward the shore.

Clarie lay back and picked up her book, but she couldn't read for wondering what Brian had in mind now. By a pure effort of self-control she didn't rush downstairs as soon as he came in. She listened to him clattering about, washing up, getting something to eat. When silence settled in, she allowed him a few minutes, and then went down.

He was reading as he ate and didn't look up. "Hi," she said cheerfully. "You get them sold all right?"

"No," he growled and stared harder at the page. His ears reddened.

"What happened?" She went over to the counter and cut a piece of applesauce cake. "They full up?"

"They've gone. Went this morning. So forget it."

She was sorry for him now in his humiliation after his big scene on the car. "You haven't opened Owen's present yet. Look, there's mine. Isn't it handsome?"

He rolled his eyes at the parka, nodded, and went on apparently reading, but she knew he wasn't seeing the words. She slid his package toward him. "Come on, I'm dying to see what's in it."

"You open it," he grunted.

It was a cream-colored wool sweater, crossed with a broad brilliant band of geometric design, and Brian's face should have turned incandescent at the sight of it. Instead, he gave an overdone shrug.

"What'd he have to say after I left? Laughed fit to kill himself, huh?"

"I had more to say than either Mark or Owen. I was ashamed of you, but they told me to calm down."

"Sure! I'm just a kid so I'm not worth getting all hawsed up about." I must be learning tact, she thought, because I'm not going to argue with that.

"What are you going to do with the lobsters?"

114

"Leave 'em right there on the mooring for now." He slammed his book shut and shoved noisily back from the table. "I'll dump 'em before I'll sell them to him!"

"May I point out, at the risk of jolting your sensibilities, that we're in the lobster business together so I have something to say about them? I couldn't slug it out with you on the car, but we're home now—and Mother isn't."

"Well, how would *you* feel, creeping back to him and having to eat crow?"

"He wouldn't say a thing to make you feel cheap. He likes you. He says you're ambitious."

"Yeah, I'll bet." He stood looking out at the harbor, hands in pockets.

"Look, we're likely to have a howling blizzard tomorrow, and Mark can take care of those lobsters better than we can."

"The wind's supposed to come northeast, and those crates will be in the lee where they are now."

Hold back, Clarie, she told herself. Be mature. "What about after the storm?" she asked his stiff back. "Will you take them back to Brigport and sell to Tom Robey? You could have sold them to him today."

"Not after he heard me asking where the *Gypsy Queen* was. You know that sarcastic smirk of his. He'd never let me live it down." He pivoted on one heel, suddenly transfigured. "Look, there'll be some fine weather after this storm. We'll go to haul again, and take all our lobsters to the mainland ourselves. Mark gets ten cents commission on every pound he sells to the Birch Point company. If we lug our own lobsters over, we'll get the

115

extra. The fisherman always does, for bringing them right to the pound."

Clarie's determination to be poised almost went up in smoke, but she said with admirable calm, "That's a tricky course even in summer. After you get close to the land you have to run in and out among all those little islands and ledges."

"For Pete's sake, we can read a chart, can't we?"

"I know, but sometimes you can get fooled just the same. It's easy to miscalculate."

"We can take our time." His eyes were shining. He was transfigured with enthusiasm. "It's only an hour and a half from here to Birch Point. We can pick a real pretty day. Can't you see it? Blue sea, blue sky, plenty of gas, plenty of lobsters—"

She could see it. She could feel her own heart lift in response. To set out across the bay in *Sea Dancer,* to ride into the wind over seas of sapphire and jade . . . a pleasantly *light* wind, so that when they reached the complicated part they wouldn't be edged off course and miss their mark. A summer wind, she realized, with her heart dropping back again. Oh, they'd had a few such days this winter, but they were the exception. In February and March, and sometimes in April, dark clouds scudding up over a blue sky could mean snow squalls instead of rain showers. Whichever it was, it would confuse you badly if you didn't know your way.

"It sounds great," she admitted, "but I think we ought to talk to somebody about it first."

"Who, Mark? Or maybe your friend Ross!" he jeered. "Why in heck do you have to be so darned cautious?"

"We don't have to talk to a Bennett. There's Mr. Fennell, Nils Sorensen—"

He had left her, stalking into the sitting room where he began to open drawers. She knew he was getting out the charts of the coast. He brought one out to the kitchen and she leaned over his shoulder as he drew the course. "That's how the lobster smack goes. Now if we can't do that we're feeble-minded, and have no business in a boat in the first place."

"I agree, we ought to be able to. If we had an absolutely perfect day, calm enough and clear enough so we don't miss a thing and don't make any mistakes, like taking The Fates"—she pointed—"for The Sisters, and steering a direct course for Pride's Fall, which is a little too descriptive for me. And don't forget we have a mother."

Brian groaned. "She's got to get it through her head that we're in *business*. We've got a chance to earn more money for all of us, and there's no reason why we can't take our lobsters in all the time. We can save 'em up till we get ten or twelve crates." He was overjoyed again. "Can't you *see* us?"

His enthusiasm moved her, especially after the remarks he'd made that morning about being tired of lobstering. "Well," she said slowly, looking off into space. He pounced on that. "Will you side in with me to talk her into it?" He had the grace to blush. "I mean, make her see we can do it all right and we'll be safe? We can choose our day, go in the morning early before it breezes up, and promise her that if it blows in the afternoon we'll stay over till it flattens out."

"All right," Clarie conceded. Suddenly she knew that she wanted to go, if only to give Brian an incentive to keep on working. He wasn't tired, as his mother thought, but simply bored, and the trip to Birch Point with the lobsters would give him a change. "But I wouldn't say anything about it now," she warned him. "Wait till the storm's past and the weather's really nice. If she has it to think about now, it'll get to be as big a trip as crossing the Atlantic."

He grinned. "I know what you mean. Oh, man!" He smacked his fist into his palm. "Wait till they see us steaming out of the harbor loaded with crates!"

14

Aburst of springlike weather followed the storm. Coming in from hauling on the first good day, they agreed that the time had come. At supper they would bring up the subject.

If Mrs. Tanner was startled and then opposed, she didn't show it at once.

"We'll see," she said. "Do you mind if I sleep on it?"

"Gosh, we want to start early tomorrow morning right around daylight, if it's fine," said Brian, "and I want to gas up tonight, and everything."

Clarie touched his foot warningly under the table. "The next day might even be better than tomorrow. The five-day forecast is a good one."

"Oh well." He subsided, and knew enough not to bring the question up again that night. In the morning he showed a sense of duty toward his schoolwork, and Clarie industriously did some mending and ironing. By boat time their mother still hadn't given them any decision on their project, but neither of them mentioned it until she'd gone to the mail.

"I dunno why she has to be so darned long-winded about it," Brian grumbled.

"Because she's a mother," said Clarie briskly. "She has to consider all the pros and cons. And you'd better get back to work, or you'll be sliding behind again."

"Oh, who cares?" He collapsed in his chair like a dropped sack of meal. Clarie didn't bother to answer. As soon as their mother was convinced that Brian would never be happy anywhere else but on the island, being a lobsterman, she would cease to care about the schoolwork, but until then it was a point of honor with Clarie that Brian should keep up. She had assured her mother that he would, she had *promised* that he would.

And what about herself? Was she still so clear about what she wanted, now that Paul had been here and gone? It was confusing, it was frightening. She shut her eyes over her darning, and conjured up Jamie. If only you could *make* yourself fall in love! If only it didn't sneak into your life without warning! But perhaps you *could* make it happen. . . .

Brian moaned, which meant he was in English again. "How the heck can you tell the difference between who and whom? And who cares, anyway?"

"You mean, whom cares." Clarie laughed. "Just substitute *he* and *him*. You wouldn't say, To *he* are you speaking."

" 'To him are you speaking' sounds pretty silly too, but I get the point, I guess. Why don't they let us pick out our own subjects for biweekly themes?"

"That's what I always wondered, but I suppose it's a good exercise for your imagination to see what you can do with their ideas."

"*That's* going to make me a better lobsterman?"

Clarie saw her mother coming along past the fishhouses with Mrs. Caldwell. They talked by the steps a few minutes and then Mrs. Tanner came into the house, escorted by an eager Hodge. "Oh, what a Marchy wind!" she said. "Old Hodge has been prancing around like a kitten." She sorted the mail on the table, then began putting away the groceries she'd brought. Brian and Clarie gazed without speaking at her back. As if she felt the combined stare, Margaret said without looking around, "I've made up my mind. The answer is *no*."

"*What?*" Brian's voice climbed and cracked. "But you said—"

"I said, 'We'll see.'" She faced him. "I know, all small children think that when Mother says 'we'll see' they're as good as in. But neither of you are small children, and that's part of the trouble."

"Meaning?" he asked sulkily.

"Meaning that you two have more responsibility than you should have at your age, and that makes it hard for me to decide what's the best thing to do. In a lot of ways you're both pretty mature, but in other ways you're your age, and I like it that way." She smiled into his stricken face. "No, I can't let you go. You've never done it before, it's a bad course, and the weather's treacherous this time of year. Those are enough reasons, I should think."

"We'd go when it was fine, we wouldn't take any chances!"

"You've never been over the course. Ross and Mark said this morning that sometimes even the smack has trouble."

"Mother, did you ask their advice?" Clarie asked before Brian could.

"Of course I did, dear, I had to ask someone. I didn't want to keep you from doing something you wanted so much to do. Well, I *did* want to, really, but not from pure maternal silliness."

"It was family business but you went to *them*," Brian said in a low, intense voice. "Mark would tell you anything to keep us from making that extra for ourselves and Ross doesn't want us to get ahead anyway! He chases us around out there when we're hauling most of the time, just to see how much we're getting, and—"

"Brian!" His mother held up her hand. "Stop that. Mark doesn't need your lobsters to keep the wolf from his door. And he knows a lot more than you do. So does any man on the island. And I'm glad Ross chases you around when you're hauling. I don't draw an easy breath from the time you go out of that harbor until you come back into it. I let you go just the same because I appreciate what you're doing. But I *don't* have to let you make this foolish unnecessary trip just because you're mad with Mark."

"Mother, nobody's mad with Mark," said Clarie. "But we could use the extra money, that's all."

"The extra money wouldn't pay for the wear and tear on me. I don't believe your sense of self-reliance will be permanently crippled because I'm putting my foot down on it. I'm entitled to make noises like a mother once in a while, and that's what I'm doing. Mark will buy your lobsters whenever you take them over to him." She put up her hand again. "No more discussion, please."

122

"I wouldn't be caught dead towing those crates across the harbor!" Brian stamped out of the house.

"We could've done it all right," Clarie murmured. "It's poor visibility, and the tide taking you off course, that gives trouble. We know that."

"I said no more discussion, Clarie," her mother said gently.

"But just tell me one thing, and I won't say anything more. If they'd said we could do it all right, provided we used common sense, would you have let us go?"

"Yes, I might have let you go. A person should use the advice she asks for. But I wouldn't have been happy about it."

"Till we called from Birch Point in an hour and a half. . . . Mother, we're five, six, and seven hours out to haul!"

"But you're always in view of somebody, and besides, you know these waters as you do this house. Even then I can't help being anxious. But I try not to burden you with it." She looked into the girl's eyes. "My confidence took a terrible beating last year, Clarie."

"I know that." Clarie was instantly, wretchedly ashamed. "Well, if Brian won't take the lobsters over, I will."

"You tell Brian from me that he's to row those crates across the harbor."

"Don't make him, Mother. He had his heart set on this, and he's in such a state he's better off alone. I'd like to get out and row."

123

It was noon, and a quiet time, with the children and women inside for dinner. The mailboat had left. She went across the road to the wharf, wondering where Brian had gone. She could see her mother's viewpoint, she was remorseful because her stubborn attitude had forced her mother to explain it. But equally strong was her own frustration. Everything could go to pieces all at once and then what would she do? She fumbled at the skiff painter with suddenly frantic fingers.

There were five crates tailing off the empty mooring now, and she untied the line from the buoy and fastened it to the rope becket in the stern of the skiff. This was the little lull that meant the wind was about to change. The harbor was the light sunny blue of a moire hair-ribbon Clarie had once loved. It even had the same shimmering grain. The sun beat strongly through her heavy jacket and she took it off. In the lee of Mark's wharf it was as warm as summer. She was kneeling on the car making the string of crates fast to a post when she heard the thud of feet coming down the wharf.

"Well, here they are," she said curtly.

"Now that's what I'd call a good mess of lobsters." It was Ross on the ladder, not Mark. He smiled at her and shoved his cap back on his head.

She stood up and faced him. "Where's Mark?"

"He'll be along." He took hold of one of the crates and slid it onto the car and across the boards to the scales. He had no jacket on, and wore a new wool shirt of muted plaid. His work pants were as well pressed and fitted as neatly as most men's dress slacks. Dapper Dan,

124

she thought scornfully. Showing off. She knew she was being childish, but there was a sort of chilly comfort in disdain. "Where's your brother?" he asked as he reached for the next crate.

"I don't know," she said coldly.

"You don't think he's gone and jumped off Fern Cliff in despair, do you?"

"I suppose it's funny to you," she said, "but maybe your interference has made some real trouble for my family. We could have made that trip all right, and convinced my mother, if you and Mark hadn't put your oar in."

He straightened up from the crates and looked at her quizzically. "Look, do I know what you're talking about? It sounds like something pretty drastic to me."

"It *is* drastic," she rushed on. "And it could be fatal to the way we live. What right do you have to meddle? Nobody asked you to be our guardian! It was important to us to do this. It was necessary. You don't know how much it meant to Brian. Why, he's so worked up he's likely to quit altogether!"

"Would that be so bad, Clarie?"

"It would be terrible!"

"For him? For your mother? Or for you?" The soft words flicked at her like small flames, but before she could cry out against them he said, "Look, if you feel this strong about it, I'll go in to Birch Point in company with you. That way Brian can do what he's set on, and still your mother won't worry. She could even go along with me if she wanted to." His dark eyes held her in one place like a pair of strong hands. There was no escaping them. Humiliation piled on humiliation.

"Is that your idea of a joke?"

"No, I'm dead serious. I never had any idea you kids wanted to go so much."

"You kids," she repeated bitterly. "Yes, I'm a kid too, like Brian. That's all we ever were to you, a couple of wrong-headed brats playing at a man's work, a pair of nuisances everybody has to watch over—"

"I'm sorry, Clarie," he said. "I shouldn't have said that. No, you're not a kid, but do you know it?"

"Of course I know it!"

"How much else do you know?" His unhurried voice pursued her.

"I know what you think!" she burst out. It was like a bad dream, all the violence spilling out into the tranquil sun-washed noon. "That we wouldn't let our mother sell the boat or the gear, so our traps are set around in everybody's way. And when we want to strike out on our own, it has to be stopped because we aren't fit, we don't know anything, we haven't got the sense God gave little green apples! You'd like it, wouldn't you, if we folded up because of this and had to go away!"

"No, I wouldn't like to see you go away. If you think that, Clarie—" He stopped and looked out over the harbor. Then he shook his head as if answering an unheard question, and turned back to her, speaking gently. "Even if nobody kept you from taking your lobsters to Birch Point, the end could still be in sight. Sure, you two are doing a man's work. But you're a girl, and

126

Brian's a skinny youngster with a lot of growing to do. And your mother's under a strain. How long did you think you could keep on ruling the roost, Clarie?"

This *was* a bad dream. "You don't have any right to talk that way," she protested. "And we don't have to stay here where people like you are trying to run our lives. I can take my mother and brother to Brigport, or even farther away, to some place where people will leave us alone."

His smile was odd. Seeing it, she was appalled for an instant, as if she'd done something terrible without knowing what. Her throat seemed to close. Then he said, "Maybe all your mother and brother want is for you to leave them alone."

He turned away from her and went up the ladder and along the wharf. She heard his footsteps die away in the sunny silence. She put clammy hands against her hot face, then knelt swiftly and untied the skiff, and rowed away with such frantic haste that the oars kept coming out of the oarlocks.

She rowed straight back to the Tanner wharf, went into the fishhouse and upstairs into the loft. It smelled of rope, of wood smoke and salt, and its two windows were thick with dust and cobwebs. She sat down on a pile of old nets and hugged her knees up under her chin. *How long did you think you could keep on ruling the roost, Clarie?* Was that how she appeared to him? How could she ever look at him again? And what was that other horrible thing he'd said? *Maybe all your mother and brother want is for you to leave them alone.*

127

As if I were some kind of female tyrant, she thought. A dictator. Or one of those egomaniacs who goes into a tantrum whenever she's crossed, so everyone's afraid to make a scene. "I'm not any of those things," she whispered fiercely. "I'm *not*."

If only she could find out if her mother and Brian had such secret thoughts about her. Not Brian, she reflected grimly; he says everything he thinks about me. All those irritated queries and retorts ceased to be a younger brother's natural speech and took on a piercing significance. As for her mother ... how many times had Clarie changed the subject, made excuses, and argued so passionately that Margaret had given in?

Her mother had once been armored against the most vehement arguments, but now she was weakened and tired in many ways, and very lonely. What Clarie had done, she knew now, was to take advantage of her mother's low point as a small child does, knowing to the final degree just how far to go.

She had to cry out in self-defense, "But somebody had to think for us! Maybe I don't always know what's best for everybody, but this time I did. And I *still* do!" She bounded to her feet. This business today wasn't anything at all but a show of temper on Brian's part because he couldn't have his own way—and on her part too, she'd admit it—and nothing else. She'd seen it as earth-shaking, she'd made the violence, but it really had been no more than a family argument until Ross began to meddle. Who did he think he was, anyway? *How much else do you know, Clarie?* Foolishness!

128

She ran down the steps and out of doors. Hodge came out from under the building and she gathered him up and carried him home.

"Oh, to be on Bennett's, Hodgy," she said to him, "now that April's here, or going to be here shortly, sure as preachin'."

Brian was there, lying on the couch and reading. He looked the same as usual. The table was set. "At last," said Mrs. Tanner with a welcoming smile, "we can eat. For some reason I'm starved this noon."

"Why didn't you start eating Brian? His ears look nice and tender." Washing her hands at the sink, Clarie felt her spirits begin to soar in reaction from their plunge to the depths.

"How much did we get for the lobsters?" Brian asked.

"I don't know yet. Mark wasn't around the wharf, so I just tied the crates up and left them." Why in the midst of this pleasant rebound did she hear Ross's footsteps dying away into silence?

15

A FEW NIGHTS later Clarie came awake with a start that was unpleasantly familiar. So she had awakened night after night after her father died, to see the light shining dimly up the stairs, and she'd known that her mother was down in the kitchen, unable to sleep, unable to escape her thoughts. Her heartbeat speeding up with alarm, Clarie went downstairs in bare feet. Her mother was sitting by the table, reading, an ice bag held to one cheek.

She blinked at the apparition of Clarie, and then gave her a haggard, one-sided smile. "Yes, it's ulcerating. I should have gone in long ago, don't tell me."

"I'm not saying a word," Clarie protested. "I just wish I could do something for you."

"I don't know why these things always strike at night. It'll probably stop around five in the morning."

"Will it bother you if I get something to eat?"

"Nothing," said her mother, "can possibly bother me any more than I'm being bothered at this minute. Just —don't—*clash* anything."

Clarie fixed a mug-up of cocoa and bread and butter. To know that someone near her was enduring intense discomfort always preoccupied her, as if she were trying by concentration to take some of the pain to herself. So now her sympathy for her mother pushed everything else to the utmost rim of her mind. They sat there in silence for a time. When she carried her dishes to the sink her mother said, "You don't have to sit up with me, dear. Go back to bed and go to sleep. This will stop when it's of a mind to."

"All right, but if you're asleep when I get up, nobody's going to wake you," Clarie promised. Upstairs she bundled Hodge to the foot of the bed and climbed in. Hodge promptly moved up again, and his purr against her back washed over her like distant surf and put drowsing words into her head, pictures to match. ... Wonderful. ... *We shall see, while above us/ The waves roar and whirl,/ A ceiling of amber,/ A pavement of pearl.* What came next? Quick, before the roar and whirl of the waves drowned the memory. ... *Singing 'Here came a mortal,/ But faithless was she!'* No, it should be faithless was *he*, faithless was Paul. And it was Margaret who was left, and Clarie was left too. ... *And alone dwell forever.* ... The distant surf swept her into sleep.

She awoke all at once, and knew by the strong sunlight across the harbor that it was late, at least for her. But they'd hauled through yesterday, and she sank back deliciously free of the need to rush. Besides, it was Sunday.

Then she heard sounds from downstairs and remembered her mother's toothache. If she'd finally got to bed and to sleep, Brian should be more careful. She pulled on her robe and went down, but it was her mother there in the kitchen. She was dressed, her eyes looked more rested, but one side of her face was definitely swollen and she was cautiously sipping coffee.

"It stopped at last," she said. "What bliss! I went to sleep as if I'd been drugged. But I'm going to Limerock today. I think Dr. Stanley will be able to squeeze me in somewhere tomorrow."

"Good, but who's going in today?"

"Owen and Laurie are, she told me yesterday. He has to have his hand checked on, and he's taking Laurie and the children, since it's vacation. The teacher's going too."

"Well, I'm glad you're going to have that tooth looked after, instead of waiting till Next Time," said Clarie sternly.

"And if you have any errands you want done, make a list for me. I won't wake up Brian. He can call me at the Harley House if he wants anything." She looked thoughtfully at Clarie. "I'd like to ask you not to go out to haul while I'm gone, but I suppose that would be an insult to a couple of salty old professionals. Yet I'd know you weren't out on the ocean if it started to blow hard, or snow."

"Fat chance of that," said Clarie. "Ross has chased us home more than once before we were ready because he felt a snowflake. Talk about Chicken Little!"

"Thank God for Ross, then, and all the rest of them who don't mind speaking up. Well, I shall get packed. They're leaving at nine."

Brian slept on. Hodge, in from his morning walk, lay solidly curled against his back. "He looks about ten," said Margaret Tanner as she came away from his door. "I suppose when he's getting married he'll look all of fourteen to me, and I'll go all sentimental and teary."

"If you do I'll disown you," said Clarie, "and your daughter-in-law will hate you." They laughed softly on their way downstairs. At the foot Mrs. Tanner said seriously, "You know that if Brian gets overtired he gets picky. Just leave him alone, don't argue, don't push, even if it means giving up a day's hauling."

Clarie didn't protest. What happened after her mother was gone was strictly between her and Brian. But she didn't intend to miss any good days to haul. They walked around to Mark's wharf to meet the others.

Mark and his wife and little boy were on the wharf to see them off. And Ross. The usual self-consciousness attacked Clarie at sight of him. It infuriated her and she thought, Why does *he* have to be hanging around here? Peter greeted her as an old friend, and she couldn't hurt Ross's feelings by refusing to speak to him, but her nod was stiff.

"Mother, be sure and keep the scarf over that side of your face," she said. I suppose he thinks that's being bossy, she thought. It's a good thing he's got no family, or he'd be busy ignoring them all the time and never get anything else done. She wished Miss Colwell a pleasant vacation at her home near Portland. "Brian had better do a little work this week," the teacher warned her. "He'll tell you it's vacation—I know all his arguments, and he can be very persuasive." She smiled. "Lots of charm."

"He'll work," Clarie promised.

"I've laid it all out for him. It shouldn't be enough to

make him feel abused, but if he doesn't do it he'll start backsliding again, and I'd hate to see that."

"I'll tie him to the desk." They both laughed.

"Ross, you be sure to make Buff stay in nights!" Holly Bennett called anxiously. Her little brother chimed in with the name of his cat, and Ross solemnly promised each one that meals and bedtimes would be properly observed.

"I see where we could hire a good cat-sitter if we ever needed one for Hodge," Margaret Tanner called up to Clarie, who refused to smile.

After the departure Clarie didn't linger around the store for conversation, but went straight home. The effect of the encounter with Ross over the lobster crates was still with her, and whenever she remembered the interlude in the fishhouse loft she hastily changed the subject. But you couldn't keep changing the subject forever.... At least where Jamie was concerned there were no doubts or illusions, and she didn't have to question herself about her own behavior there.

Brian got up toward noon and said at once, "Why didn't somebody wake me up? I could have gone too. I'd like to see some movies." He brightened. "Hey, maybe I'll go in on the Tuesday boat! Why don't you go too?" he asked generously. "Linnie'll feed Hodge."

"Thank you muchly," said Clarie, "but I think we'll stay home and tend to business."

He was putting his breakfast on the table, a concoction of scrambled eggs and cheese and ketchup that only he could stomach, and he straightened up and stared icily at her. "Got your whip all limbered up, I see. Got the leg irons out. Simon Legree, she was known as in them days."

"Oh, for heaven's sake, sit down and eat and save the drama," Clarie said good-naturedly. "Mother hasn't even got to Limerock yet, and we're at it."

"Well, *I* didn't start it," he said with dignity, "and if you think I'm spending this week with my nose to the grindstone you're nuts. If I was in school I'd at least have my vacation." He began to eat. It was the first time he had ever mentioned school in such a way. The threat was strong in the room; let him say this once in their mother's hearing, and that would be the end.

With great self-control Clarie went back to reading her book. He didn't go on with the argument either.

The rest of Sunday passed pleasantly. They each went about their own affairs, and didn't discuss any sensitive subjects when they met at supper time. This was a kind of picnic, since Brian liked large unmanageable sandwiches filled with many ingredients, and Clarie cooked up a cheese and tomato dish which she liked and nobody else did. After supper they went up to the Percies' where Ralph, Joey, and Hugo were getting together for some music. They came home all sung out and feeling very friendly toward one another.

Maybe the momentum of this would carry them through tomorrow, Clarie hoped as she got ready for bed. Because we've got to go on, she thought passionately. We've got to show everybody that I was right.

16

S HE WASN'T surprised when Brian was slow
getting started the next morning. She
swallowed her sarcastic comments. Maybe I'm lucky at
that, she thought. If it wasn't fit to go to haul I'd have to
get him started on his lessons. Her confident assurances
to Miss Colwell now seemed foolishly optimistic. As he
got ready to go out, his movements were all slow-motion,
his hands and feet might have been made of wood, and he
wore a sulky, evasive look.

The clouds had a look of early spring to them, and as
usual when *Sea Dancer* was taking the crests with the
light gay motion that gave her her name, Clarie cheered
up and hoped Brian would do the same. The time they
spent together in the boat was the best time. I'll always
remember it and I hope he will too, she thought with a
tinge of unexpected sadness.

The lobsters had slacked off even more, and Brian's
face grew longer. He began shoving traps overboard
without taking care how he set them. Clarie's good reso-
lutions went at last.

"For heaven's sake, that one's probably standing on
end down there!" she cried at him. "You act as if you
never put a trap overboard in your life before. Haul and
dump, haul and dump, that's all you're doing."

"What else is there to do? No lobsters, we're just
changing the water in 'em, that's all."

"No matter, we still take care of our gear. You haven't even been putting on fresh bait! If you don't want to do it right, let me do it." His shoulders went up almost to his ears.

"O.K., Cap'n Bligh. She's all yours." He stripped off the cotton gloves and gazed indifferently through the windshield. In a fury she grabbed the gaff and said, "Get going then. We haven't got all day."

He reached down to speed up the engine and it stopped completely. The silence was great. The boat rocked lazily, the water made cheerful little sounds around the hull. With a martyred look Brian went through the starting procedure, but nothing happened except a straining whine. They looked at each other with shared consternation. The engine had never let them down yet; it couldn't be doing so now. Brian tried again. Nothing.

"Flooded," said Clarie tersely. "Wait a minute." They sat on the engine box and tried to wait. But after that there was still nothing.

"Well, looks like she's up and died on us," said Brian. "Good thing it's not blowing a gale or we'd fetch up on the Seal Rocks before we could get an anchor out."

"Speaking of anchors," said Clarie, and went scrabbling into the storage space under the stern. She brought it out with its accompanying coil of rope and looked at it doubtfully. "Looks pretty small to hold us in one place," she said.

"It'll hold if there are enough rocks down there for it

to catch on. Hope to heck it's not all sandy bottom."
They checked the line and tossed the anchor overboard.
There was a moment of suspense, but finally the line came
taut and they knew the anchor was hooked.

Now there was nothing to do but wait until somebody
noticed them. There were other boats in sight, though
not close by. They ate their lunches and conjectured on
the nature of the trouble. Once in a while one of them
tried to start the engine, but soon they gave that up.

"I wouldn't even mind old Granny Grunt coming
along, right now," said Brian. He took the top off the
engine box and studied the contents. "Could be the
carburetor, could be the gas line fouled up, could be
something's really gone. I hope it's something Mr. Fennell can fix. Brother, if I had his knack I'd have me a
machine shop and haul in the dough hand over fist."

"I guess he could make a business out of it if he wanted
to," Clarie agreed. Now is the time we should talk about
ourselves and what we're doing, she thought. But for
once she didn't know how to begin. It never used to matter. She simply started, and if Brian didn't like her ap-
proach she was prepared to outtalk him, outshout him if
she had to. But there ought to be an easier way. . . . She
watched him as he went back for more lunch. The easy
way to find out anything was to ask the direct question,
like: Brian, are you really tired of lobstering? Brian,
would you really rather be in school with the other boys,
instead of doing lessons alone and having the boat and
the ocean and island life?

It didn't seem as if the answer to the last question
could be *yes*. It just couldn't be. Yet she was afraid to

138

ask him. They wondered if their mother had seen the dentist yet, talked about the news they'd heard on the radio that morning about Vietnam, Cuba, the Common Market. It was quite a conversation, but they never once touched on family affairs.

"Hey, we're saved!" Brian said, and pointed. "Whaddya know, it's not the Gestapo! Don't tell me he's deserted us."

It was Joey Caldwell who came up alongside. "Need a horse?" he said with a broad grin. He took *Sea Dancer* in tow and left her beside her own wharf. There was no chance of settling Brian down to schoolwork this afternoon; like Clarie he was worried about the engine, and when he saw Mr. Fennell coming in, he went around to meet him.

Mr. Fennell went home for dinner and then came back to the Tanner wharf. Brian stayed with him while he worked on the engine, handing him tools, watching, asking questions. As the tide ebbed and left the boat they made sure the beached hull would stay on even keel by piling a dozen or so heavy rocks on the washboard next to the wharf, so that the boat would list that way, against the wharf, and thus stay upright.

Clarie spent the afternoon helping Marjorie Percy paper her spare bedroom. For a break they took milk and cake out onto the back doorstep. Ralph came home and said the engine trouble was caused by the carburetor; Charles Bennett had a spare one and Mr. Fennell was installing it right now. "So you're all set, Cap'n," he told Clarie. "You can go down to the sea again, to the call of the running tide and all that jazz." He took one of her

139

hands. "You getting to be one of those horny-handed sons of toil? I mean daughters."

"Not if gloves and gallons of hand cream mean anything."

Ralph stroked her hand and rolled his eyes. "Pretty smooth, pretty smooth! And all being wasted on the desert air."

"My, we're full of quotations this afternoon, aren't we?" said Marjorie. "And Clarie's hand isn't being wasted, to judge by the way you're holding it."

"Well, I think somebody should be holding it."

"I understand there are several candidates for the job," said Marjorie. "We all know about Jamie. Then there's—" She stopped, and Clarie said, "There's who?"

Marjorie's shrug was too casual. "Well, we do have a couple of youngish bachelors on this island and there are a few over on Brigport too. Not to mention that dashing character in the tight pants who came out here to see you. You underestimate yourself, Clarie," she said seriously. "All you have to do is wave those long lashes of yours in the right direction—"

"Now don't go putting her up to any of those tricks," said Ralph. "I like her lashes fine the way they are now."

"But you're taken, dear," said Marjorie gently. "And how do you suppose I got you? Let's go back to papering."

Clarie went home in a good mood. She'd suggest helping Brian with one or two of his lessons tonight. That might make it more interesting for him. She made an upside-down cake of gingerbread and peaches to follow

140

the lobster chowder she'd put together when they got home this morning. You see, Mother? she said silently. I'm not pushing. I'm being tactful. *Mature*. And Brian will respond.

Brian, grease-daubed, full of professional chatter about engines, scrubbed up and managed to keep on talking throughout the process. His favorite meal disappeared in large quantities, and Brian still talked. Clarie waited with benign patience for him to run down, which would surely happen when a full stomach had its inevitable effect. Instead Brian sprang up from the table saying, "Good supper, Sis. Leave the dishes and I'll help you with 'em later. I'm going up to Hugo's."

"You are not," said Clarie flatly. "We're going to do some schoolwork."

"Maybe *you* are." He was already half into his jacket. "Be my guest."

Patience, Clarie, she told herself. Maturity. "Brian, look, an hour's work tonight, with me helping you, will cut way down on your work tomorrow."

"Who's working tomorrow? This is vacation week!"

"You've had your vacation, all the days when you skinned out with your gun or went to Brigport with somebody, or hung around in somebody's fishhouse."

He grinned, made a rude noise, and ducked out the door. She pulled it open behind him. "You be back in this house by nine-thirty," she called, "or I'll come there after you."

There was no answer from the dark, and the surge on the harbor shore drowned the sound of his feet going

141

away. It had grown very cold after the seeming mildness of the afternoon. Hodge cried somewhere out of sight and she waited for him to come, hugging herself and shivering, but not with cold. Loneliness? For the first time she thought of Ralph and Marjorie almost with envy. They had each other and the island, with no one asking them inconvenient questions or making them feel confused and guilty. *Each other.*

As she cleared up the dishes she wondered if Jamie would come. But then he wouldn't know that she was alone in the house, and he wouldn't want to make conversation around Brian. She got out some knitting on which she had worked at irregular intervals, found a radio discussion on extrasensory perception, and tried to settle down.

Brian came home a little after nine-thirty. He'd been afraid she'd show up at the Bennetts' and even if he'd refused to go home with her he still would have looked a fool. "Breezing up northwest," he said curtly as he took off his boots. "We can't leave the boat at the wharf all night."

"What time is it high tide?" Clarie read the tide calendar between the two front windows. "Two-thirty-five, take off a half-hour for the difference between here and Boston—two-five. How about if I set the alarm for quarter of two?"

He nodded and went upstairs. She followed shortly and set the alarm on her small bedside clock. No use giving him one, he could sleep right through it. On second thoughts she set the alarm for five minutes earlier, to

142

allow for rousing him. It was a nuisance to have to get up and go out in the middle of a winter night, but they couldn't leave the boat there to pound against the spilings in what might turn out to be a hard northwest blow. And as far as the dark was concerned, there was no difference between seven in the evening and two in the morning.

It had been a long day and in spite of her depression she went quickly to sleep. As the tide came back to the harbor ledges, small explosions of spray burst and gleamed in the darkness, and swift miniature rapids of foam raced through the seams and crevices, but nobody was there to see.

17

As usual, she woke just before the alarm clock went off. Never had her bed been so warm and soft; never had her legs and arms and head been so heavy. Fighting against sleep she crawled out into the chilly air, gathered up her clothes and flashlight, and went into Brian's room. Hodge stayed behind in the nest of bedclothes, purring luxuriously.

Brian didn't respond to a mere word. She had to shake him and he muttered and groaned and tried to turn over to escape her. But she kept talking. "The boat, remember, Brian? We have to take the boat off. Come on!"

At last he said coherently, "Be right down."

She lit a small lamp and dressed by the kitchen range. "Brian!" she called from the foot of the stair, and heard a thump. She set his rubber boots in front of the stove and brought the oilclothes in from the entry. "I'm warming your boots!" she shouted, and began to get into her outdoor clothes. When she was ready, she heard him on the stairs and called out, "I'm too hot. I've got to go out. I'll go along to the wharf."

"Okay," he answered thickly. "Don't start untying anything till I get there."

"You think I'm nuts?" she asked amiably.

The oilclothes were wind-cutters, and with a knitted

144

cap over her ears she felt the cold only on her face. The air revived her, and she looked up at the stars. A whole new set had moved overhead since nine o'clock.

Once she thought she heard an engine, but the illusion was swallowed up by the loud swash of water all around the harbor shore. There were no lights anywhere. When she went out onto the wharf the beam of the strong five-cell flashlight revealed *Sea Dancer* surging against her ropes. Dashes of spray flew over the buff paint.

Brian hadn't come yet, and already it seemed as if she'd been out here for a long time. The tide was high enough so that she could step easily down onto the stern deck. Well, at least she could warm up the engine while she waited. There was a little lull when the boat lay still, and she jumped down. In one searing moment, as her right foot went out from under her, she knew that spray had been freezing on the deck.

The flashlight flew out of her hand and bounced down into the cockpit, she was shooting off the glazed deck, her legs out over the splashing black water. She was squirming to turn over, clawing for something to hold onto. One frantic hand finally hooked around the stern bit, and the wild slide was halted. She lay on her stomach, her feet out over the side, her cheek scraped against the icy deck, her breath making sobbing sounds, her eyes tightly shut.

The pounding in her ears increased, and became the sound of feet running down the wharf. There was a thud as someone landed beside her.

145

"What are you doing down here alone?" The man was quietly enraged, and it was not Brian. Cautiously she rose up onto her hands and knees, and saw Ross's face in the dim glow of the dropped flashlight.

"It *would* have to be you, wouldn't it?" She laughed weakly. "You always come along in time to see me take a header, even if you have to wait up till two in the morning for it."

"You break anything?" Ross said. "No? Have you been overboard?"

"I think one foot went under." She crawled down into the cockpit and sat on the engine box, feeling sick.

"You could have drowned," he said.

"I didn't have that in mind," she assured him, hoping she wouldn't throw up while he was there. "I was just going to start the engine while I waited for Brian, and there was ice on the deck. What are you doing at the harbor this time of night?"

"I had to put my boat off. She was in at Charles's wharf. I happened to look this way when I started home, and I saw the beam from a light shoot through the air as if somebody'd thrown it."

"That must have been when I hit," she said feebly. "Well, I guess I owe you an apology, and some thanks too. If I'd gone overboard, you'd have been here in time to haul me back alive."

"I might not have got here in time," he said. For some reason he was calmly but profoundly angry. She could feel it. Because I'm a nuisance, she thought in dreary shame, and I don't blame him. "Where's your brother?" he asked.

"He should be here. He was coming downstairs when I came out." She was shaking inside her clothes with reaction. "He's so d-darned slow, he's probably eating. I'll go get him—"

"*No.*" He held her arm hard. "That would be two of you to go overboard next time. You go home and to bed. I'll tend the boat."

She was still staring at death, too preoccupied for pride. "I'll wait," she said. "No, I'll go with you."

"I don't want you. One of us to get into a dancing skiff is enough. Get up into the fishhouse." He hoisted her up by the elbows, gave her another lift to the wharf; for some reason her hands were weak when she tried to pull herself up by them. "Here. Take your flashlight, I've got my own."

She went and stood inside the fishhouse doorway. Brian must be eating and reading, having lost all track of time or else decided that it was good enough for her and her bossy ways to have to wait for him. When she told him that she could have slipped overboard and drowned, he would only say that she shouldn't have been in such a hurry.

Ross started the engine, cast off the lines and left the wharf. Their skiff was already on the mooring. I won't tell Brian what I did, she thought drearily. But he'll be along in a minute, and find out that Ross is doing our job for us because he doesn't consider us responsible,

147

and we've just proved that we aren't. . . . It seemed to her that never, even in the time right after her father died, had she felt the oppression of defeat that she felt now, at two-thirty on a February morning, as she stood inside the dark fishhouse.

A bit of ice was to blame. If it hadn't been for that, she would have had the engine started by now, and then gone back up to the house to roust Brian out. She would be a different person, as different as sunlight from fog, summer from winter.

Still Brian didn't come, and the splashing around the wharf spilings and ledges had swallowed up the sound of the engine. Of course Ross would be on the mooring now, making *Sea Dancer* secure. But was that a splash, a cry, a little rag of sound? Could you hear it in here?

She stepped outside and flashed her light out across the water. It caught one dancing boat after another, and finally *Sea Dancer* on her mooring, alone.

The wind was picking up; the chug on the shore growing louder. She strained so hard to see something else that her eyes stung and began to water. If there'd been frozen spray on the stern deck, there was frozen spray on the bow deck.

The boat could lurch just once and catch Ross slightly off balance. He could slip overboard, and how long before she knew what had happened? By then it would be too late for help. She knew with a deathly sickness in her stomach, in her whole body, that the coincidence *could* happen. The news was full of such things. She fought down rising nausea, and flashed the light back and forth across the water between the moorings and the shore.

Where would she go to wake someone up, to tell them that Ross was drowned out there in the harbor and it was her fault? She couldn't bear it. She had borne everything else without breaking, but this was too much. She sank down onto the doorstep and wept into her hands. It was not the easy business that loosens the tight nerves and relieves body and soul. She had cried once like this, alone in the woods, when her father died. She remembered the dreadful similarity. She'd never cried like this for Paul, because even without her Paul was alive and enjoying life. So had her father loved his life, and so must Ross in his quiet way. She saw him with his dog, or solemnly promising to take care of the children's cats; at the wheel of his boat, or standing looking off across the sea as if he could never have enough of it. She saw his rare smile, and this cut through her with a twisting blade. Her sobs wrenched at her stomach, shook her body.

When she realized that someone was standing over her, she thought it was Brian. Mopping her face with a sodden handkerchief she said in a thick, hiccuppy voice, "He's out there! G-get somebody—"

"Who's out there, Clarie? *Who?*" Ross sat down beside her and put his arm around her. She sagged against him in a flood-tide of relief that washed away the last of her pride. "I thought you'd d-drowned," she stammered. "It was all my fault."

"Oh, what a girl," he said softly. He rocked her against

149

his chest. "Flooding the fishhouse. You're washing everything right out the door. A buoy near hit me in the eye when I came up the ladder."

She kept her face against his jacket, knowing she should thank him and rush home with dignity intact, except that dignity had been washed out of the fishhouse along with the buoys. She couldn't look him in the face, and this seemed the handiest way to avoid it. Besides, there was such a wonderful relief in not fighting, in being weak and boneless and infantile, and being held while she felt all those things. He was like a rock in his strength. You realized all at once that nothing could happen to him. Nothing *must*. . . . Startled at the direction of her thoughts, she braced back and he pulled her close again.

"It's all right," he murmured as if calming a child. "It's all right."

"It *would* have been all my fault," she insisted in a muffled voice. "And the worst of it was that I couldn't think what to *do!* I just sat there and bawled!"

"I'm glad you did. I don't think anybody ever bawled about me before."

"But don't you see?" She straightened up and tried to see his face in the icy starlight. "I've made a fool of myself tonight. Brian's let me down, we've shown everybody that we're just what they said we were, and I nearly killed you into the bargain."

"You did not nearly kill me. I tied the boat off, that's all. Same as I did to my own. And I'm not everybody, but thanks."

"Maybe I don't mean everybody. Maybe I mean—"

She stopped. The storm was quite over now. She said in an almost normal tone, "Thank you for doing it, anyway. And I know I'll never again jump aboard a boat like that unless it's summer, bone-dry, and broad daylight."

"Remember that. I was never in any danger, but you were. So be careful. You don't belong just to yourself, you know."

"Yes, I know," she said humbly. "And while I'm feeling so meek I'd better apologize for the way I acted on the car that day. I was just plain awful."

"Fiery," he said solemnly. "Nothing wishy-washy about you." He still had one arm around her. It was strange in one way, but still not strange at all. It would need pondering at another time, in another place. It must have been the reaction from everything else that made it so hard for her to make an energetic move.

The fishhouse windows rattled suddenly in a strong gust, and she said, "I'd better go home."

"You can sleep late," he said. "It'll be no day to haul."

"So we have schoolwork." But at this moment she couldn't care less. She made the effort finally, and he stood up with her.

"Are you wobbly?" he asked.

She started to say No, then was honest. "Yes. But I hate to admit it."

"Don't be so proud."

He walked with his arm around her across the road and to the end of the walk. The faint light from the windows shone on their faces. She had the alien fancy that if she looked closely at him he would appear different to her, but she did not look. She said, "Well, thank you again."

He took his arm away. "Don't be too hard on Brian." If he was smiling she couldn't tell without looking at him. "Good night, Clarie."

"Good night, Ross." He was gone, and she still hadn't looked at him. The dark and the water and the rising wind wiped out his voice and his footsteps.

She narrowed her eyes against the dim light in the kitchen and saw Brian on the couch. Half into his oilclothes, he had fallen over onto his side and was sleeping heavily. She moved softly toward him, staring.

He looked as if he had been struck down from behind. One hand still held laxly a strap of his oilpants. He *had* been struck down, by sleep. It was so deep that she could hardly see him breathe.

She had never really looked this closely at Brian before. It was a fantastic experience. He was there, and yet not there, defenseless, oblivious, and mysterious—he was not the bundle of prejudices, enthusiasms, impulses and reactions known to her as Brian up to now. He was *someone else,* whom she didn't know, who was the center of his own universe as she was the center of hers.

Each of us, she thought in astonishment, stands at the center, *our* center, and life spins around us. Other people exist only as their life brushes against us in the spin, or collides. Then you get either fusion or disaster.

Still watching her brother in his sleep, she began taking off her outdoor clothes. The warmth of the room caught up with her and she was ready to sleep herself. Brian should be in his bed, but could she wake him enough to start him upstairs? Cautiously she swung his legs up onto the couch, and he still didn't wake, even when she pulled off the long-legged boots and the stiff yellow overalls. He was coming to the wharf, she thought, but he was just too tired. He couldn't make it. Mother was right. Everybody's been right but Clarie. Clarie could've killed him tonight, if she'd managed to drive him down there, as clumsy as he'd have been. Maybe it would have been a good thing for everybody if Clarie hadn't got a handhold when she skidded.

No, that was a kiddish thing to say. It wouldn't have helped anything or anybody—it would have put a dreadful burden on both her mother and Brian, who would have thought he was responsible. She covered him with a blanket, blew out the lamp, and went upstairs. People always thought of violent dramatic gestures instead of the simple obvious ones because they didn't want to bow to the simple and obvious. But she had no choice.

18

WHEN SHE woke up in the morning it was well after eight. It didn't matter. The day stretched before her in brilliant windswept vacancy, all her sense of urgency and drive had departed. She dressed languidly and went downstairs. Brian was up, had made oatmeal, and was setting the table. He looked tight and worried.

"Who took the boat off?" he fired at her. "You didn't do it alone, did you? I wouldn't put it past you."

"Oh, relax. While I was waiting for you, Ross Bennett came along. He had his boat in, remember?"

He was less taut, but angry now. "He put her out for you? Why in heck didn't you come back and haul me out? What'd you let him do it for?"

She splashed cold water on her face. "If you knew how you looked last night, you'd know why I let him."

"I didn't mean to conk out." He was honestly bewildered and repentant. "I felt so darned groggy I could hardly move, but I was pulling on my oilpants . . . at least I remember starting to put them on . . . and that's all. I woke up on the couch this morning with Hodge standing on my chest, and I thought he was a tiger, for Pete's sake!"

"Old Hodge would be flattered. And don't carry on about the boat. Anybody as tired as you were shouldn't be dragged out in the middle of the night. You'd have been a menace to yourself and me too."

"What did he have to say?"

"Nothing much."

"Didn't he tell you this proved something or other?"

"All he said was that today would be no day to haul, and he's right. What are you going to do?"

Taken by surprise he gave her a wary look across the table, and then proceeded cautiously, as if expecting her to break in any moment and remind him of lessons. "Well, uh, I should patch pots, but—uh—Matt and I thought we might go looking for seabirds down in Pond Cove, and—"

"All right." She said nothing more. Let him wonder; she hadn't even the energy to tell him that today nothing mattered, even the schoolwork upon which she'd expended so much passion. She wanted only to be left alone and have peace in which to reassemble herself. After last night she felt thoroughly disintegrated.

When he had gone she faced the facts with an honesty so unsparing she couldn't understand how she had escaped so long. "That took some talent," she told Hodge, bleakly. "Maybe that's where my real gift lies." Yet to say it in so many words, to admit surrender—who wouldn't avoid it for as long as possible? She walked up and down the sunny kitchen. Whenever she faced the windows she saw *Sea Dancer* bobbing at her mooring on dark sapphire water flecked with white. Hodge sat in the rocker and purred noisily.

"Brian will fight now, for all he's been grousing about

too much work.   But it won't matter how much he fights.
School is where he belongs.   As for me—" No, not the
shop.   Not Paul.   Never Paul.   She knew that now.   But
what?   Here was where the clinging came in, the desper-
ate reluctance to give in, give up.   She could not see herself turning into the other Clarie, and yet it had to happen.   She only hoped that everyone would have the de-
cency to say "I told you so" in the privacy of his home and
not to her.

She couldn't stand the house, so she went around to the
store to call her mother at the Harley House.   The bad
tooth was out and the dentist would remove the stitches
tomorrow.   Her jaw was only slightly tender.

When Clarie left the store she met Jamie.   "Hi," he
said with a grin.   "I saw you start over, so I've been lying
in wait.   My mother wants you and Brian to come up
and have supper tonight."

"We'd like that."

"Want to go for a walk this afternoon?"

"If I'm going out for supper, Jamie, I'll have to get a
nap.   We got up at two to take the boat off, and I didn't
sleep very well afterward."

"Well, I can walk you to the doorstep," he said cheerfully.

She relented and said, "Come on in and have a mug-up
with me.   I don't even remember my breakfast."

He was pleased, and she was glad she had asked him in,
because he began telling her some island history that his
uncles had been discussing last night.   She asked ques-

156

tions and kept the talk on this safe subject for an hour. He ate four doughnuts and drank two mugs of coffee. Finally he looked at the clock and hit his forehead. "I'm suppose to be building pots! It's a wonder my father hasn't come after me."

They parted in laughter, but the bleakness came back when he had gone. It was the hanging-on part that was bad, this marking time until her mother came back and she could tell her what had to be said. *You were right and I was wrong. Now what do we do?*

Brian did all the talking at noon. She yawned once in a while so he'd think her silence came from sleepiness. After dinner she said, "I'm taking a nap. What are you going to do?"

"Oh . . . ." He was a little too casual, and she wondered what was coming. "I thought I'd go through a math assignment and maybe make a start on that theme. Sort of kick some ideas around."

"You're going to *study?*"

"Sure, why not?" Then he grinned. "Well, Mother's over there with that darned tooth, wondering if we're getting anything done out here and worrying about it, so I figured I ought to have something to show her."

"I know she'll appreciate it, Brian," Clarie said. "Is there anything you want me to help you with?"

"Not right now. On the grammar assignment later on, maybe. And there's a history quiz, by the way. A hundred questions and they call it a quiz, for Pete's sake."

"I remember those quizzes. Well, I'll go flop." As

157

she left the room he called after her, "Hey, I saw Ross this morning, and I thanked him, in case you're interested."

"That's good, I'm glad you did," she answered. Up in her room she lay on her bed in the afternoon sunshine and watched the scallops of light ripple across the ceiling, and thought of last night. If it hadn't been for Ross, would she have come to the point of surrender so soon? He had forced the issue without knowing it, because she had been so appalled and afraid while he was gone. It seemed as if she'd never been so afraid. The fear had cut her to the bone. And what if he *hadn't* come back, but was gone just like that, in the rise and fall of a wave?

She turned her burning face in her pillow. Until last night his name had stood for one set of impressions; now there was a new set. . . . I'll be ashamed when I meet him again, she thought. How does he see me now? As a scared and blubbering kid? . . .

Supper at the Sorensens' turned out to be fun, and she was grateful for it. There was a lot of laughter at the table, and afterward a hilarious card game in which everyone played, even Nils. They finished off with pie and milk. Once in all this time Jamie and Clarie met alone, in the kitchen. She was rinsing glasses at the sink, and Jamie came up behind her and took hold of her elbows. "Can't you send Brian home alone, and we'll go around the long way?" he asked.

Instantly she was depressed, though she tried not to show it. And why? She'd liked being with him before, and he was no different. But I am, she answered herself, and now his hands on her arms caused a wild rejection in her, so that she had to use self-control not to shrug him off.

She was saved by Linnie's dashing through on her way to the back door, shouting, "It's snowing, and Phronsie's out!"

Jamie moved away from Clarie and muttered something. Linnie came back talking baby talk to the cat in her arms, and brushing snow off her. The crystals glittered on her own head. "It's a blizzard!" she gasped dramatically.

"It's just a cloud going over," Jamie said. But when they got ready to go it was still snowing thickly, with great flakes blown wildly about by a strong and variable wind.

"I'll see you tomorrow," Jamie growled under cover of the general conversation at the door. She nodded. Tomorrow was another day, she didn't have to think about it tonight.

19

T HE SNOW merely spread a sparkling glaze
over everything, and in the morning sun
it soon melted away. The old snow was going quickly
too in the mild salt air. By noon the paths were muddy.

Brian and Clarie were both up early and out to haul.
After a few days ashore he had more color in his face
and seemed anxious to tend the gear. Clarie listened to
his cheerful comments with sadness gnawing at her. I
hope he always remembers these days, she thought, because when we break this up it will be the end. Even if
we're all living together for years to come, we'll still be
going separate ways, in separate lives. And we'll start
out on those separate ways as soon as Mother comes back.

But I'm only nineteen! she argued against the corrosive
depression. I shouldn't be thinking about ends, but
about beginnings! The island will always be home to us,
we can come whenever it's possible. . . . But it wouldn't
be the same then as being *part* of the island, having your
life on it, knowing you'd never have to be homesick for
it again. And was there anything worse than being homesick for a place while you were still in it?

"What's the matter with you?" Brian teased her.
"You're blue as a whetstone."

"Oh, there's nothing wrong with me that a few brains
won't help."

She kept a resolutely optimistic expression for the rest of the time. When they came in, *White Lady* was tied up at Mark's wharf, and Owen was on the lobster car with his brother.

"Well, I guess the doctor's satisfied his stitches are holding," he greeted them. "I'm out of retirement."

"Congratulations, Commodore!" Brian had conceived a special liking for Owen on the day of the accident.

"I know we thanked you for our presents the other day," said Clarie, "but I didn't have a chance to tell you how much I liked the color of mine."

"Well, now, it was easy picking. I just had to remember what color your eyes were." Then he burst out laughing. "I'd like to be a liar, but the gift's not in me, so I can't take the credit. I was supposed to be lying around with my arm in a sling that first afternoon, so I got Ross to do my buying for me. He came back to the room and showed me, and I said, 'How come you're so good at remembering that girl's eyes?' And *he* said, " 'How come you're so sure that's the color?' "

He and Mark were immensely amused. Clarie felt herself blushing. It was ridiculous, but she couldn't stop it.

"Hey, what color in my sweater is supposed to match my eyes?" demanded Brian. "The red or the yellow?"

"You blend them and get orange," said Clarie. "Brian the Orange-eyed Sailor. We'd better get out of the way, here come two more boats." One was *Moonlight*.

"Your mother came home with us!" Owen called as Brian started the engine.

"Good!" Brian shouted back. "I'm tired of Clarie's cooking!"

The kitchen smelled deliciously of pot roast, and Margaret Tanner was whipping cream. The swelling had gone from her face, she'd had her dark hair cut in a new way, and she looked so young that both her children were startled. You get to thinking of her as *Mother,* Clarie reflected; you forget she's *Margaret,* and pretty, and not yet forty.

She had brought back, among other things, a box of the chocolate eclairs they all liked. While they ate these with milk she told them about her trip. She'd managed to do a good many things in three days besides visiting the dentist. When they'd finished eating, she told them that she had done even more.

"There's no quick and easy way to get around this," she said quietly. "But you both must know that I've never really been happy about this arrangement. I've given you your own heads, because I thought it might help you to work things out after your father died. At least that's what I told myself. But I'm afraid the truth is that I was too taken up with my own misery to insist on our doing the right and sensible thing."

Brian was sitting very still; it was impossible to tell by his expression what he was thinking. Clarie couldn't sort out her own thoughts.

"I guess I needed to get away so I could look at things in the proper perspective, without either of my children to argue me down," she said with a smile. "Owen says he's out of retirement. Well, I am too, and I intend to be in charge of this family for a while yet. This isn't to say I'm not proud of what you two have done, because I am. But you've done it long enough, and you're both getting worn out."

Brian came upright. "Whaddya mean, worn out?"

She shook her head. "No more arguments, Brian, at least about this. I have a job promised, and I've found us a flat. It's a nice one, the whole top floor of one of those old mansions on the hill. You don't feel shut in at all, and you have a wonderful view of the whole bay. Brian's to start school next Wednesday, because we're going in on the Tuesday boat."

Her cheeks attractively pink, she sat back and contemplated her children. They contemplated her. Clarie didn't know if she was relieved, dismayed, or simply numb. It had all been taken out of her hands. But it was so horribly *final*.

"I won't start in the middle of the year!" Brian burst out. "I'll be behind, I won't know the kids—"

"You know the ones from Brigport, and besides, you make friends quickly. And the teachers will bring you up fast on your work. I've talked with the principal."

"He's not behind," Clarie said. "At least not much." We're actually going, she thought, and so *soon*. She felt hideously vacant in spite of two eclairs.

"If you can't get all the traps up this week," her mother said, "somebody else will see to it. I talked with Owen on the way out."

163

"Are you going to sell the traps and the boat?" Brian was out of his chair, clutching white-knuckled at the back of it.

She smiled at him. "Brian, the boat is yours and Clarie's, as far as I'm concerned. You've earned the right to say what to do with her. You can spend your summers lobstering out here, if that's what you want. And if, when you finish high school, you want to be a lobsterman, I won't stand in your way. But you're to have your schooling first."

He didn't answer, but his grip loosened on the back of the chair. Now that he wasn't worried about the boat, things would sort out quickly for Brian. He would be quite happy in the stream of school life by the end of another month, even though he would always have the island in the back of his mind.

"Well, Clarie?" said her mother. "What are you thinking?"

"Nothing much, except that you're probably right. I guess it had to come." She forced a smile. "Tell us about your job."

"Well, it's a good one. Dr. Stanley pointed me to it. It's with the Benner Insurance Agency, and it won't actually start until next September, when the girl who has it now is getting married. They want someone older, who will stay with them, and I'm it." She smiled. "I'll have time to work on my typing and shorthand this spring, and of course we'll have this summer free to come back out here."

"You'll be free, you and Brian," Clarie said quietly. "I'll have to look for a job myself."

"Paul wants you back at the shop," Brian suggested.

"I don't want to go back there." She got up and said with false cheerfulness, "Well, anyway, I don't have to think about it right now. My gosh, there's an awful lot of work to do around here."

"It doesn't have to be done all at once. We can come out in the April vacation to tie up loose ends."

"What about Hodge?" Brian asked suddenly.

"Hodge is old, and he's always been with us. He doesn't travel so far afield now, and I think he'll settle down in the flat all right, as long as he's with us. There's a nice fenced-in yard, so he can get his feet on the ground, and oh, yes—" Her smile lighted her face. "Mrs. Brownlee says they've never been able to get the mice out of the attic. So Hodge can have a job over there too. And in the summers, after I'm working, he and Brian can come out and keep bachelor's hall."

Brian grinned at the picture. "That's that, then. I guess I'd better put the boat off on the mooring." He went out, and they heard his usual joyous whistling.

"He'll be all right," said his mother. "What about you?"

"I'm all right too," Clarie said strongly. After all, she owed her mother something, and the *something* was some adult behavior. "The main thing is the job. I don't want to go back to the shop because of Paul. Otherwise I'd love it, I always did. But it was on account of Paul that I left it. I mean I—" She fumbled for words under her mother's questioning eyes. "I did want to be home here . . . you know how I've always felt about the island. I did want us to be all together here after Father went. But it was Paul who triggered it. He's the reason why I dared to think Brian and I could manage the gear together, so I suppose I really owe him some thanks." She gave her mother a wry smile. This was less painful than she'd ever expected it would be; Paul was growing smaller and smaller, a figure seen through the wrong end of a telescope.

"We were supposed to be in love. He was going to come out with me on my vacation and get to know the island and the family, and you'd get to know him, and—" She shrugged, and spread out her hands. "Well, he had second thoughts, that's all."

"Oh, Clarie, it must have been so hard for you, and I never guessed," her mother said softly.

"Well, it's over. Really over." Her mouth quirked. "He had third thoughts and showed up out here, but to no avail, as they say in books."

"You were probably wise. He's charming, but he doesn't sound very stable. Well, Clarie, you needn't rush to find a job, you know. You've earned a good bit of money since you started lobstering, and you deserve some time to yourself. You might even take some courses at the high school adult education classes while you're looking around."

"Yes, I could." Clarie looked as if she were considering it. "But there's something else I'd like to do first."

"Name it. You've been so reasonable that I'm ready to say *yes* to just about anything, so don't take advantage of my weakened condition."

They both laughed. "Well, it's not much. I mean, nothing really drastic. I'd just like to stay out here by myself for a couple of weeks. I could do some cleaning and putting away, and so forth. Otherwise we'd spend all Brian's April vacation housecleaning."

"You can stay if you want to, and you can bring Hodge in when you come." She got up to fix the vegetables for supper.

"I'll take your suitcase upstairs for you," Clarie said. She put it in her mother's room and then went to her own and sat down on the edge of the bed. She felt light-headed, trembly in her arms and legs. So much had happened all at once that she hadn't yet caught up with herself. She looked forward with fervent hope toward the breathing spell she had won. Her mother was satisfied that she understood the situation; but how little she really knew! And I don't know much more, Clarie thought, except that I've never been in such a state in my life.

20

CLARIE SAW her mother and Brian off at noon on Tuesday. The time had gone by in a rush, with no little gaps for thinking and brooding. Brian had insisted that he and she bring in the traps, and they worked until the three hundred wet traps were stacked in long rows on the wharf and around the fish-house, each with its buoy and coiled warp put inside. Brian was cheerful for the most part, and she knew he was fortifying himself by the prospects of a week in April and then the summer vacation. When she joined him and their mother in a few weeks he would already know a good many people in Limerock, and only his mother's firm hand would keep his social life from interfering with his schoolwork.

The Tanners were invited out to supper every night of the last five days, and Margaret was pleased and touched. "This place is my home now," she said at the Sorensens'. "It became home the day when Ed and I first landed here."

"You'll be back here to live some day," Joanna assured her. "We'll totter around in our old age together."

When they left on Tuesday, the rush was abruptly ended, and Clarie felt like a strand of rockweed left high and dry on a ledge after a storm. As she walked away from the wharf, Marjorie Percy joined her.

"Come on up and spend the afternoon with me," she invited.

"Can I make it another day?" Clarie asked. "I've been tearing around so fast that once I sit down I'll probably go into a coma."

"Tomorrow then. That is, if Ralph goes out. Look, if it's as nice as this, how about taking something to eat down to Sou-west Point?"

"Sounds good. That'll give me an incentive to clean cupboards first, or wash curtains." She heard her voice as if it were coming from outside the vacuum in which she moved. They parted, Marjorie to take the little path along the edge of the woods and Clarie to follow the harbor shore.

If Ralph goes out. No matter how beautiful it was, she and Brian wouldn't be out there. She looked out across the harbor at *Sea Dancer,* alone at her mooring in the fine weather, and she didn't know exactly how to define what she felt. She supposed that sooner or later something recognizable and probably painful would attack her.

In the house she wondered where to start first. Well, there were the dishes from breakfast and lunch. She washed them, then lay down on the kitchen couch to look at the magazines that had come. Hodge lay beside her. The clock ticked hypnotically on, the pattern of sunshine moved slowly on the floor as the earth turned, and she fell asleep.

When she woke up she thought first that her mother and Brian were in the house and it was morning—time to

169

get started out to haul. She could hear the engines warming up in the frosty sunrise. Then she came fully awake and realized everything. Her heart beat in heavy, slow rhythm, and she felt a stubborn and sickening sense of loss, like the grief one feels in dreams. It seemed to have no connection with her mother and Brian and the end of their life here. It was something personal to her, Clarie.

She washed her face in cold water. This took away the drugged sensation, but the strange grief still remained. She went to the windows and saw that the first boats were coming in; it was their engines she had heard. One was Nils Sorensen's boat, and she could see Jamie looking this way. He knew she was alone, and he'd be around to see her as soon as he was ashore and washed up.

She took her jacket, went hurriedly out the back door, and took a short cut she hadn't used for years, ever since she'd outgrown the playhouse on the knoll behind the house. The path led around the playhouse site and into the strip of woods at the foot of the Bennett meadow. Once there, she went rapidly across the meadow and down into Goose Cove. She hated to run away from Jamie like this. But to say *no* to him today would be worse than running away from him, because she had no logical reason to say it, and she couldn't make glib excuses, and he would be hurt. He was going to be hurt soon enough, anyway.

She walked more slowly as the distance increased between her and the harbor. At last she came to the steep little cove where she had sat and cried on that freezing January day. The log was still there. "Here sat Resignation on a Stump," she said aloud. "There ought to be a plaque on this log. Maybe I can make one out of a tin can." She sat down and began skimming flat stones across the lustrous blue-green water.

"Now what did you wake up in such a mood for?" she lectured herself. "Take stock. You're healthy, intelligent, you get along with your family, you've got over Paul, you can take your time to find a job that suits you. . . . All that should be ailing you is leaving the island, and that shouldn't be tearing you to pieces. Of course you don't *like* it, but if you're a sane and reasonably mature human being you accept the inevitable with as much grace as possible. And if that isn't a lovely speech you're nuts. I think I'll engrave it on my plaque, if I can find a tin can big enough."

Something moved behind her, and it wasn't the wind stirring the low-sweeping spruce branches. She turned her head and looked into the amber eyes of Peter. Nose to nose, she and the dog contemplated one another. Then Ross came down from the woods and stood there looking at them.

"What are *you* doing here?" she said flatly.

"That's what you said before, remember?"

"Are you still humoring Peter?" She tried to sound sarcastic, but failed.

"No, this time I'm humoring me. Mind if I sit down?" He sat down anyway. She fought an impulse to get up and run, and clamped her hands around her knees.

"I thought you were out to haul." She tried to skip another stone and failed.

"I came in early," he said. "I don't mind admitting I'm sly. I saw you from Charles's shop when you left the house and skinned out the back way." He was leisurely with his pipe, looking up now and then to scan the horizon with narrowed dark eyes. "So I followed you. On the mainland you could call a policeman, but we're outside the law."

She laughed to make herself sound gaily puzzled. "But why did you follow me? If it's about the boat or the gear—"

He laid his pipe down on the beach stones and looked squarely into her face. "Clarie," he said in the most quiet voice possible. "I'm not interested in the boat or the gear, and you know that. If you ever let your mind come to roost long enough in one spot, you'd know even more."

Heat surrounded her so that even her eyes were hot, and she had to will them not to blink. The beach stones were dazzling. "Maybe you'd better explain," she said huskily. Her lips wanted to tremble.

"Why do you think I've followed you and Brian so closely? It was more than being neighborly. There were plenty of others to keep an eye on you." He unclamped her fingers one by one from her knees. For all that she was so warm, her hands felt clammy between his. Deep inside her a wild recognition was struggling to break free. It couldn't be, and yet it *was*.... It was growing stronger every moment, with great beatings of its wings—an osprey striving to soar.

"You know now, don't you, Clarie?" he asked. "I'm a

172

proud man, too proud. I wouldn't run the risk of being snubbed, but every time you went out of that harbor I thought, what if something happens and I never see her again?" He rubbed her hands. "They're cold."

The grief that had awakened her, the sense of loss, the deep and most secret disturbance for so long; they were all a part of the incredible whole.

"And now you'll be going away, unless I stop you." He smiled at her. But I always liked his smile, she thought. Even when he made me mad I liked his smile. *Liked?* It cut me through, and that's more than *liking*. And why could he make me so mad? Maybe it wasn't that at all. Maybe it was something else.

"What are you thinking?" he said. "What's going on behind those eyes? You're not a child, Clarie. For heaven's sake, don't act like one."

"No," she said slowly, thinking out loud. "I'm not a child. I think maybe I've been refusing to admit it. There's always been something about you that upset me, and I've called it everything else but what it really was."

She was suddenly wonderfully serene all at once, because it was *out,* as simply as this. Paul was so tiny now as to be practically nonexistent. What had been between them was a typical boy-girl love affair . . . that was why his later talk of marriage had seemed so meaningless. By then she had come to know Ross, and he had become a part of her life—an influence which she had refused to recognize until now.

"You could always make me uncomfortable," she said.

173

"I'd come away from you all shaken up, as if something tremendous had grabbed me by the scruff of the neck and shook me till I was out of breath and sense. That's not a very romantic picture, is it?"

"No, but it's better than romantic, it's true. We have these other pictures we go by until something either grabs us by the scruff or punches us in the stomach." He took her gently by the shoulders and looked into her face. "I love you."

"I love you," she answered. The dog lying on the beach lifted his head and looked at them, and then lay back again with a deep sigh. They both laughed, and she moved quite naturally into Ross's arms.

"I want to marry you," he said.

"Yes." I adore him, she thought in astonishment. There were no doubts, no reservations. What was between them was no longer the frightening unknown, but a life. They kissed, and Paul disappeared completely— for good.

"Can we keep it to ourselves for a little while?" she asked him. "So we can have a chance to get used to it before anyone else knows?"

He nodded. "That's the way I'd like it too. We've got a lot of getting acquainted to do, and you've a name to be taken care of. I won't come to the house. I've waited until now, I can wait a bit more."

"The only thing is, how can we stay apart?" Now that she had found him she didn't want to leave him again, ever.

"It won't be for long." She could tell by his voice that

174

he was smiling, and she wanted to see his smile, but her head was too comfortable on his shoulder. "Just till I'm sure you're marrying me and not the island."

"You've seen through me," she said drowsily. She turned her face to meet his lips again. Then she sat up abruptly. "That night when you put the boat off for me, I thought I wasn't ever going to see you again, and it nearly killed me. Now when you go out to haul I'm going to go through it all over again, every time."

"That's love, darlin' mine," said Ross. "What's Clarie stand for? I always wanted to know."

"Clarissa. Isn't it awful?"

"Nope." He held her off and they gazed solemnly into each other's eyes. "Hello, Clarissa," he said. "Welcome home."

"To the ceiling of amber," she said," and the pavement of pearl."

"To *what?*"

"I'll show it to you in a book. You don't know how much it's responsible for." She chuckled. It was, even to her, a rich and contented sound.

About the Author

Elisabeth Ogilvie, well-known novelist, is the author of seven other books for young people, *How Wide the Heart, Becky's Island, Turn Around Twice, The Fabulous Year, Blueberry Summer, The Young Islanders,* and *Whistle for a Wind,* and many adult books, including *There May Be Heaven, Call Home the Heart, The Witch Door, High Tide at Noon, Storm Tide, The Ebbing Tide,* and *The Dawning of the Day.*

Born, raised, and educated in Massachusetts, Miss Ogilvie decided upon two things while still in high school: to be an author and to live in Maine. An island in the mouth of the historic St. George River, below Thomaston, is her year-round home. Her hobbies, which keep her busy when she is not writing, are children, animals, boats, gardening, reading, music, and—of course—Maine.